THE HORSESHOE TRILOGIES

Last Hope

Read all the books in the Horseshoe Trilogies:

Book #1: Keeping Faith
Book #2: Last Hope

COMING SOON:

Book #3: Sweet Charity

Last Hope
by
Lucy Daniels

SCHOLASTIC INC.

New York Toronto London Auckland Sydney
Mexico City New Delhi Hong Kong Buenos Aires

ISBN 0-439-43438-6

Text copyright © 1999 by Working Partners Limited.
Illustrations copyright © 2002 by Tristan Elwell.
All rights reserved.
Published by Scholastic Inc., 557 Broadway, New York, NY 10012,
by arrangement with Hyperion Books for Children,
an imprint of Disney Children's Book Group, LLC.
The Horseshoe Trilogies is a trademark of Disney Enterprises, Inc.
SCHOLASTIC and associated logos are trademarks and/or
registered trademarks of Scholastic Inc.

12 11 10 9 8 7 6 5 4 3 2   2 3 4 5 6 7/0

Printed in the U.S.A.   40

First Scholastic printing, October 2002

To Eva Melin—a perfect friend

CHAPTER ONE

Josie Grace shaded her eyes from the bright sunlight as she looked over at the blue car parked in the far corner of the yard at Grace's Riding Stables. "Are you sure that's Sarah's car, Mom?" she asked. "Why isn't she getting out?"

"I have no idea," said Mary Grace, walking up beside her daughter, "but that's definitely the Butlers. I wish they'd hurry up! Hope's all tacked up in her stall, and Felicity's ready and waiting for Charity. Could you do me a big favor and find out what the problem is while we get started in the ring? We're going to be behind if I don't begin the lesson soon, and Tom's coming to shoe all the horses in an hour."

"I'll do my best," said Josie.

"Thanks, dear! See you in a minute," her mother replied. She turned back to a blond-haired girl who was busy trying to stop the gray horse she was riding from taking a sneaky nibble at one of the hanging baskets by the office door.

"I hope so," Josie called, beginning to walk toward the Butlers' car. She could hear the sound of voices as she approached—Sarah's high and determined, and her mother's lower, pleading murmur. What was going on? Sarah had been coming regularly to the stables for the last year, but she'd now missed four lessons in a row. Each week, her mother had called to say that she was very busy at school and couldn't make her usual Tuesday afternoon lessons. Although she was here now, it looked as though Sarah still wasn't very happy.

When Josie reached the car, Mrs. Butler wound down her window. "Hello, Josie," she said apologetically, with a harassed expression on her face. "I'm sorry about this. Sarah's just coming—"

"No, I'm *not* coming!" Sarah said furiously from the passenger seat.

Tucking her dark auburn hair behind one ear,

Josie crouched down by the car and looked across at the sulky nine-year-old. "Why not, Sarah?" she asked. "I thought you enjoyed your riding lessons. We've got Hope saddled up and waiting for you."

"I don't want to ride Hope!" Sarah burst out. "If I can't have Faith, I don't want to ride at all."

"Sarah!" her mother said through gritted teeth, beginning to lose patience. "We've been over this a hundred times. I've told you—Faith's not here! The Graces have sold her. You have to ride Hope."

"But I don't like her!" Sarah retorted.

"Why not?" Josie asked. "Hope's wonderful! She'll do exactly what you tell her, and she won't ever run away with you or go too fast. Honestly, I bet you'll really enjoy the lesson. You'll never find out unless you try."

Sarah stared at Josie stubbornly. "I just don't like Hope," she repeated. "I don't like the way she looks."

"What difference does that make?" Josie replied, starting to feel upset herself. "It's the way she rides that matters."

Mrs. Butler let out an angry sigh and drummed her fingers on the car steering wheel, while Sarah folded her arms and stared straight ahead. Oh, this is hopeless, Josie said to herself. We're not getting anywhere. She racked her brains and tried to remember what she knew about Sarah Butler. She'd been coming to the stables for ten months or so, hadn't she? She could manage a sitting and rising trot, but as far as Josie could recall, that was about it.

"Never mind," Josie said, sitting back on her heels and looking over toward the yard. "If you really don't want to ride, Sarah, we can't force you. It's a shame, though. I was talking to Mom just now, and she said she thought you could start cantering today. Still, maybe some other time . . ."

"Cantering?" Sarah said, her eyes lighting up in spite of herself. "I thought your mother said I wouldn't be ready to do that for a while."

"Not on Faith, maybe," Josie replied, saying the first thing that came into her head—even if it was rather unfair to Faith. "But Hope's so steady, we thought you'd be fine. Oh, well, I suppose I'd better go and untack her now." She got up, brushing some dirt from the ground off her jeans. "See you around, then," she said as casually as she could, beginning to walk back toward the row of stalls on one side of the yard. It took all the determination she had not to look back and see whether Sarah would follow her. Would the gamble pay off?

And then she heard the sound of a car door opening. "Wait for me!" Sarah called. "Can I ride Hope, please? If that's still all right . . ."

Josie turned around. "Of course it is," she said with a grin. "Come on, or the lesson will be finished before you've gotten into the ring."

Hope was looking over the top half of the stable door. She gave a little whinny when she saw them coming, and shook her head so that the bridle jangled. Josie saw Sarah smile, and felt a little more kindly toward her. All the same, she still couldn't understand how anyone could turn their nose up at Hope. Maybe she wasn't the prettiest horse in the world, with her broad back and bent nose, but she had to be one of the gentlest. Her sweet, steady nature made her the perfect ride for a novice like Sarah.

Josie unbolted the stall door and led Hope across the yard to the mounting block. "She'll always stand quietly," she said encouragingly while Sarah pulled herself up into the saddle. "I think you're both going to get along really well."

"Sorry, Hope," Sarah said, patting the horse's gray neck as she gathered up the reins. "I didn't mean to be rude about you."

"Come on," Josie said as she led the way toward the outdoor schooling ring. "I'll just remind Mom about what we said."

She was praying that her mother wouldn't think she was taking over the lesson. Luckily, although Mrs. Grace looked surprised when Josie mentioned the cantering, she didn't object.

"Okay," she said. "Just fall in behind Felicity on Charity, Sarah, and we can start practicing your sitting trot. Let's not waste any more time!"

"So, what was that all about?" Mrs. Grace asked Josie as they waved good-bye to the Butlers at the end of the lesson. "Why was Sarah so late?"

"She said she didn't want to ride Hope," Josie answered. "She doesn't like the way she looks. But she realized by the end of the lesson how silly she'd been, didn't she?" she added, patting Hope affectionately.

"Yes," said Mrs. Grace thoughtfully. "She did really well today, and she loved cantering—though I must admit, I wasn't planning on letting her try for another couple of lessons."

"Sorry, Mom," Josie said, running up the stirrup and beginning to unbuckle Hope's girth. "It was the only thing I could think of to get her out of the car." She heaved the saddle off and took it over to the tack room while her mother held the two horses.

"Is something wrong?" she asked on the way back, noticing her mother's anxious expression. "You look really worried all of a sudden."

"Oh, it's probably nothing." Mrs. Grace sighed. "Hearing what Sarah said about Hope just makes me feel a little bit uneasy and sad, that's all. Remember the advertisement for her goes in the paper tomorrow?"

"Yes, I know," Josie said more grimly, tackling Charity's saddle. "I've been trying not to think about it."

"Well, I hope that we don't get the same reaction from anyone who is interested in buying her," Mrs. Grace went on. "People do judge by appearances and—let's face it—Hope isn't the best-looking horse in the world."

"Oh, Mom!" Josie protested over her shoulder as she made her second journey to the tack room. "She's wonderful! Everybody knows that."

"Everybody who knows her, knows she's wonderful," Mrs. Grace continued when Josie had come back, "but someone who doesn't, won't simply take our word for it. Our best bet might be to go for a child who's been having lessons on Hope. But I've been asking around and I haven't had any takers so far."

"Oh, I hate this!" Josie said suddenly, looping the reins over Hope's neck and starting to lead her back off to the stall. "I can't bear having to look for someone to take Hope away. I wish we could all stay here forever, exactly like we are now!"

"I know, I know," her mother said soothingly. "I feel the same way, believe me, but that's life. Grace's Stables have got to close, and we'll just have to make the best of it."

Josie experienced the same wave of shock that always came over her when she thought about the future. She found it so hard to believe that the stables were really closing. Her mother had opened them fourteen years ago, two years before Josie was born, and she'd lived all her life surrounded by horses and the horses that were boarded—the "hotel guests," as her father called them. She'd taken it for granted that things would go on in the same way forever, but then the old lady who owned the stables and School Farm—the cottage in which the Graces lived—had died. Her nephew had inherited the land, and he'd decided to sell the property for development. Now Josie and her parents had a limited amount of time to find new homes for the horses and for themselves. Faith, the elderly bay mare who had been at Grace's Stables from the very beginning, had left the month before, and now it was Hope's turn. Her daughter, Charity, would be the last to go.

"There's no way we won't find a good home for Hope," Josie said as she led her into the stall. "There's got to be someone who will see what a great first horse she'd make."

"Well, we'll just have to wait and see," said her mother, tying Charity to a ring on the wall outside. "Could you pick her feet out, dear, before Tom gets here? I'll do Charity. Connie and Tubber are ready and waiting."

The two remaining horses that were boarded with Mrs. Grace were standing with their heads over the half stable doors, watching all the comings and goings in the yard. Captain, a temperamental chestnut gelding, had already been moved to another yard in the nearby town of Littlehaven.

For a while Josie and her mother worked together quietly, making sure both horses' feet were ready for the farrier. Tom Crooke had been looking after the horses and horses at the stables since the beginning, and he knew their feet so well that he was able to make their shoes back at his forge. He only had to bring along a portable anvil, in case any minor adjustments needed to be made before they were nailed on.

"There!" Josie said eventually, straightening up. "She's just perfect. Aren't you, Hope?" she added, rubbing the horse's nose. "How could anyone resist you? I think you're gorgeous!"

"At least there's no sign of sweet itch at the moment," said Mrs. Grace, looking along the crest of Hope's mane. "That's one thing to be thankful for. She looks so much prettier when her mane's a good length."

Hope was plagued during the summer by sweet itch, an allergy to gnat bites. Grayish spots would appear around her mane and tail, and she would rub or bite bald patches as she tried to find some relief from the infuriating itching. When the rash was at its worst, she would sometimes rub away the hair on her head, too, so that the black skin underneath showed through.

"Waiting until it's dark before we turn her out in the field does seem to help," Josie said.

"And we should keep going with the insect repellent, too," Mrs. Grace said, looking across the yard as a battered black van drew up. "Oh, here's Tom. Come on, let's go and say hello."

By the time they had greeted the farrier and were walking back toward the stalls together, Hope had stretched her head over the stable door and was nibbling along Charity's back and withers.

"Oh, there she goes, grooming again." Mrs. Grace smiled affectionately. "She has to make sure Charity's looking her best."

"Well, that's mothers for you," Tom chuckled, setting up the anvil. "They're all the same. I'll get started on Charity. Won't take me too long to get them all done, will it?"

"No, only four of them waiting for you today," Mrs. Grace said. "Now, if you don't mind, Tom, I just need to make a couple of phone calls. I'll be down in the office if you need me."

"Oh, we'll be fine. I've got my assistant here, haven't I?" Tom said, smiling at Josie. She almost always helped Tom whenever he came to the stables and, by now, she knew exactly how he liked to work.

"So," he said, hammering up the nails in Charity's old shoe, "do you miss Faith? Do you know how she is?"

"Oh, she's really happy," Josie said, standing ready to pass him the pincers. "I went to see her last weekend and she's looking great. She's sharing the field with this great big black horse called Midnight, and he follows her around everywhere like a little lamb."

"And how's Jill coping?" Tom said, taking the pincers from Josie and levering off the shoe. "I used to look after her chestnut horse, Marmalade, you know. She was so upset when he had to be sold."

Jill Atterbury, Faith's new owner, had been involved in a car crash and broken her hip so badly that she wasn't able to ride. She missed having a horse desperately, though. When her parents had seen Mrs. Grace's advertisement about an elderly mare needing a loving home, they'd thought looking after Faith might be just what Jill needed to help her get over the accident. The horse had been about to retire from the stables anyway and didn't need much exercising, so the old mare would be perfect if Jill was able to start some gentle riding again in the future.

"Jill's fine," Josie said, watching as Tom trimmed Charity's foot with a pair of nippers and then rasped it flat with a file. "She spends ages grooming Faith, and she's started taking her out for walks. It's really great to see them both together. Faith slows right down to make sure Jill can keep up with her."

"She's a nice girl," Tom said, holding the new shoe against Charity's foot to see how it fitted. "I don't think you could have done better for Faith."

"If only we could be as lucky with Hope," Josie said, looking at the horse's sweet, plain face watching them from inside her stall. "It's her turn next. Mom's worried that we won't find anyone who'll want her."

"She's no oil painting, that's for sure," Tom said, following her gaze, "but she'd be perfect for a beginner. She's gentle as a lamb." He began to nail the shoe on to Charity's hoof, adding, "You'll be sorry to see her go, but what can't be cured must be endured, as my mother used to say."

"I know," Josie said ruefully. "I've begun to find that out."

"Well, that's me done," Tom said, packing his tools away an hour or so later. He'd put new shoes on Charity and Hope, but Connie and Tubber just needed their feet trimming and the old shoes put back on. "So their owners won't need to pay so much," he told Mrs. Grace when she came over from the office. "That should make 'em happy."

"They won't be getting many more bills from me, anyway," she said. "These two are both leaving in a couple of weeks."

Josie crossed over to the stall and gave Tubber's patchy coat a gentle stroke. She wasn't quite as close to the boarded horses as she was to the Grace's own horses, but, even so, life would seem very strange without them. They were part of the furniture, like the hens that clucked around the barn or the ducks that waddled to and from the pond next to the schooling ring.

"Where are they going, then?" Tom asked, undoing his leather apron.

"They'll both be joining Captain at the stable in Littlehaven," Mrs. Grace replied. "I'm going to keep on exercising Connie, though—Jane and I have worked it all out." Connie was a lovely black mare whom Mary Grace had been sharing with her owner, Jane Ramsay, for the past eight years.

"Well, best of luck to you," Tom said as he prepared to carry the tools and equipment back to his van. "I'll miss my visits here, that's for sure. Fourteen years is a long time."

"Yes, it certainly is. We only had Faith and Tubber when you first came, didn't we?" said Mrs. Grace. "Oh well, they've been fourteen good years, and now it's time to move on. Who knows what the future holds? Come on, Tom, let's go over to the office and I'll make you a cup of tea. I've bought some doughnuts to help cheer us up. Are you coming, Josie?"

"No, thanks, Mom. I think I'll stay up here for a

while," Josie replied. "I'll see you later."

She felt like spending some time on her own with the horses and, besides, she wanted to be busy when Tom left the yard for the last time. It would be too sad to watch him go and then just mope around, brooding.

Hope was standing quietly in her stall, nibbling at the hay. Josie picked up a brush from the kit and began to groom her with long, steady strokes, thinking back to what her mother had said. What if no one would look beyond Hope's plain appearance and see her sweet nature? What would happen then?

CHAPTER TWO

A couple of days later, Josie was sitting on a low stone ledge that ran along the ground outside the office and the tack room. Her back was against the office wall, and she was tickling Rascal, one of the Graces' two black-and-white cats, with a piece of straw. Across the yard, Charity, Hope, and Tubber were standing in their stalls, while Connie had already been turned out into the field. There was plenty to be done—sweeping, mucking out, and the never-ending chore of cleaning tack—but Josie didn't feel like working. She'd changed into leggings and a T-shirt after a busy day at school, and she was just too warm and comfortable sitting out in the sun.

Rascal rolled on his back, grasping and kicking

at the straw with all four paws before tearing it into pieces with his sharp white teeth. Then, suddenly losing interest, he curled up his tail and closed his eyes. "Silly cat," she said affectionately, rubbing the soft warm fur on his stomach. At least Rascal would be coming with them when they moved, along with his sister, Millie, and the family's mongrel terrier, Basil. Cats and dogs were easier to take than horses.

Josie yawned, shutting her eyes and resting her head on her arms against her knees. She was just dozing off when she sensed a shadow looming over her. Squinting up, she saw her friend Anna Marshall standing there, with folded arms and a smile on her face.

"Come on, lazy bones," Anna said, giving Josie's foot a little kick. "You'll get a headache if you fall asleep out here."

"Oh, Anna, leave me alone," Josie grumbled. "It was really peaceful until you came along."

"Yes, but you're all red and grumpy already," Anna said. "You're too fair to sit in the sun, Josie— you know that."

Josie held out her bare arms. "I suppose so," she said, looking at the pink flush below her T-shirt's short sleeves. "Now, if my skin was the color of yours, I could stay out here the whole day."

Anna laughed, shaking her glossy black hair, and stretched out a hand. "Come on," she said, pulling Josie to her feet. "There must be something we could do in the shade."

Josie gave a big stretch and looked at her watch. "Well," she said, "Hope needs tacking up, I suppose. Emma Price is coming for her lesson in about ten minutes."

"Perfect, then," Anna replied. "Good thing I came along, right?"

They went into the tack room. The saddles were arranged neatly on racks, and bridles hung from circular pegs on the whitewashed walls, each one labeled with its owner's name. Mrs. Grace had taken down Faith's nameplate, but the empty peg still gave Josie a pang when she saw it.

Anna unhooked Hope's bridle while Josie heaved her saddle off the rack, together with the fleecy saddle blanket that fitted underneath. They walked across the yard together.

"Hi, Ben," Josie said, spotting Anna's twin brother in another of the stalls. Ben often took

Tubber out on Thursdays after school, and he'd told Josie the day before that he'd be coming up to the stables.

"Thanks for keeping him in for me," he said, giving the horse a quick going-over with the dandy brush. "I'll just get rid of some of this dirt, and then we'll be off."

When their parents had separated three years ago, Ben and Anna had moved to the village of Northgate with their mother. On her first day at school, Anna had met Josie and discovered that she lived only a couple of miles away. She and Ben had turned up at the riding stables the next weekend, and begun to help out in exchange for free lessons. Although Ben had really been too small to ride Tubber at first, the gentle horse never took advantage of him, and they'd soon become firm friends. Mary Collins, Tubber's owner, was thankful to have some help exercising her horse during the week. She taught at the same school as Robert Grace, Josie's father. They both had tons of grading and lesson plans to cope with, so it wasn't always easy to find time for a ride.

"Where are you going?" Josie asked Ben, hoisting the heavy saddle more comfortably over her arm and looking into the shady stall. Her mother had strict rules—people going off for a ride on their own had to tell someone roughly how long they'd be gone and which route they were planning to take.

"I thought I'd go up Baker's Hill and then along the bridle path around the field and back," Ben said, putting the brush back in Tubber's grooming kit and coming around to open the stable door. "I'll be back in about an hour. Do you and Anna want to come along?"

"Hope's got a lesson now, so I think we'll just hang around here," Josie said. "Have fun!" She liked Ben, though they weren't best friends in the way that she and Anna were. He was a lot quieter than his sister, but when he did say something, it was usually worth listening to.

"Sure thing," he said, smiling at Josie as he went off to the tack room for Tubber's saddle and bridle.

Josie greeted Charity with a pat as she passed, then let herself into Hope's stall. Anna was already with her favorite horse, holding a chunk of apple out flat on her palm. She wasn't very confident on horseback, having had a bad fall once on vacation, but she trusted Hope completely and always chose to ride her.

"You'd spoil her if she wasn't so good-tempered," Josie said, watching Hope stretch out and take the apple with a delicate twitch of her lips.

"Well, I don't have much longer to make a fuss over her," Anna said, laying her face against Hope's smooth neck for a second. "Mom showed me the ad for her in yesterday's paper. Have you had any replies?"

"A couple," Josie said, starting to saddle up the pony. "One wasn't too serious, but the others are going to come see her on Saturday."

"It's strange," Anna said thoughtfully as she began to put the bridle on. "You'd have thought more children who ride her here would have been interested. Lots of them wanted to have Faith, didn't they?"

"Yes, I suppose they did," Josie replied, fighting a nagging sense of unease in her stomach. "I don't know, maybe Mom hasn't asked everyone yet." She couldn't bear to think her mother might be right—that people wouldn't want Hope because of the way she looked.

"I keep wishing there was some way she could come and live with us," Anna went on, "but unless my fairy godmother suddenly appears, I can't see how it's going to happen. She wouldn't be very happy in our little backyard."

Mrs. Grace came to the stable door, a visor cap over her dark curly hair to shade her eyes from the sun when she was in the middle of the ring. "Thanks for getting Hope ready," she said to Josie and Anna. "Emma's just arrived, so if you bring her out, we can get started."

"Hang on a minute, Mom," Josie said. "You remember how much Emma wanted to buy Faith, even though we told her Faith was too old? Well, Hope would be perfect for her! She's just the right size, and she could really help Emma learn to ride. What do you think?" She looked at her mother eagerly. "Do the Prices know we're selling her?"

"You know, I don't think I've said anything to them yet," Mrs. Grace said slowly, thinking it over. "You may have hit on something there, Josie, thanks! I'll mention it to Emma. Hope would be a good match for her!"

Josie and Anna sat together on a tree stump, watching Emma come to the end of her lesson. Mrs. Grace had gotten her trotting without stirrups, which were crossed over the front of Hope's saddle and lying on her withers.

"But w-w-why are we d-d-doing this?" Emma asked breathlessly as she jolted alarmingly from side to side.

"So that you can feel the way Hope's moving when she trots and learn to go with it," Mrs. Grace replied briskly. "That's the idea, anyway. It'll really help your seat. Do you remember what I told you about the trot? It's a walk with two beats. Hope's legs move in diagonal pairs—that means one front hoof and the opposite back one hit the ground at the same time, followed by the other pair of hooves."

"Emma's going to be stiff tomorrow," Anna said, chewing on a blade of grass.

"She looks good on Hope, though, doesn't she?" Josie commented. "They seem to be the right sort of shape for each other."

"Okay," Mrs. Grace went on, "pull gently on the reins now and go back into walk. Don't let Hope go to sleep, though! Squeeze with your legs to keep her walking on properly until you come to the letter B. Then you can turn in and halt. Well done, Emma— you've worked hard today."

She opened the gate leading out of the schooling ring, and Emma walked Hope through and back into the yard. Josie and Anna got to their feet and strolled around to meet them.

"Hi, Dad!" Emma said proudly as her father came over from his car. "Did you see me?"

"I certainly did!" he replied. "You're really coming along."

Josie held Hope and threw her mother a meaningful look, while Emma dismounted. Mrs. Grace took a deep breath. "Mr. Price," she began, "do you remember the conversation we had about you buying Faith, the horse Emma used to ride?"

"Yes," he replied, taking out his wallet and flicking through the bills. "Why do you ask?"

"Well, now we're looking for a new home for Hope," Mary Grace said, giving the horse a pat while Anna began to unsaddle her. "I just wondered whether you'd be interested? She's so quiet and steady, she'd be ideal for Emma."

Mr. Price looked at Hope for the first time. "What do *you* think?" he said to Emma. "She's not as handsome as the other one, is she?"

Emma wrinkled her nose, smoothing out the

creases in her brand-new jodhpurs. "No offense to Hope or anything, but I think I'm outgrowing her," she said. "Now that my riding's getting better, I need a horse that's a bit more lively. And I couldn't imagine taking her to a show. She's not exactly the prettiest one around, is she?"

"But she's wonderful at gymkhanas!" Josie burst out. "She does everything you tell her to and she doesn't get overexcited, or lose her head. You'd do really well with her, honestly."

"I don't think so," Mr. Price said decisively, looking at his daughter's doubtful expression. "As a matter of fact, we've been over to the riding school at Littlehaven, and Emma's going to start having lessons there. I think they'll be able to advise us on a horse for her." He held out his hand to Mrs. Grace with a bill in it. "Thanks for getting her this far, but we think she'd benefit from some more advanced teaching now. Keep the change."

"Good-bye, Mrs. Grace," Emma threw over her shoulder as she was hurried off to the car. "Thanks for everything!"

Anna, Josie, and Mary Grace watched the Prices' car sweep out of the yard. "Honestly!" Josie said angrily. "Emma doesn't realize how lucky she is! She's had one-to-one lessons on two of the nicest horses she could ever find! Her riding's only gotten better recently because Hope guesses what Emma wants her to do before she's thought of it herself."

"I think Hope's much too good for Emma Price," Anna said, giving the horse a hug. "I'm glad she's not going over there."

"But where *is* she going to go?" Mrs. Grace said anxiously. "We haven't got unlimited time on our hands to find her a new home."

"Come on, Mom!" Josie said. "Just because Emma's turned her down, it doesn't mean everyone else will. The ad only went in the paper yesterday. You can't start getting discouraged yet! There are some people coming to see her on Saturday, remember."

"Oh, I don't know," Mrs. Grace replied. "After what Sarah said, and now hearing the same kind of thing from Emma—well, I can't help but worry. What if everyone reacts like that?"

"Well, they won't," Josie replied, stamping out any worries before they had a chance to develop. "After all, you wanted her when you first saw her, didn't you? Someone else is bound to feel the same way." She stroked Hope's rippling mane. "Besides, she's looking her best at the moment. We'll find a good home for her, just wait and see!"

CHAPTER
THREE

"Mmm, it's going to be another beautiful day," Josie said, breathing in the sweet, fresh air. It was early on Saturday morning, and she and her mother were walking through the garden toward the fields that surrounded the house to start bringing in the horses. Beads of dew on the lawn sparkled in the sunshine, and everything was quiet except for the sound of birds' singing. The Graces' brown-and-white terrier, Basil, scurried along beside them, rooting about under bushes or sniffing the air eagerly in his constant search for rabbits.

"I wonder if it's going to be like this all summer?" Mrs. Grace said. "I can't believe it, the grass needs cutting again! Maybe we should look for a house with a smaller yard next time."

Josie looked back down the road at School Farm: the place where she'd lived all her life. "They're not going to knock the house down, are they?" she asked her mother. She couldn't bear the thought of School Farm being destroyed, but she didn't want to imagine anyone else living in it either.

"I don't think so," Mrs. Grace replied. "To be honest, I'm not really sure what the developers have in mind. All I know is that we have to be out by the end of July, which only gives us another six weeks or so to find somewhere new. The trouble is, your father's so busy with this musical that we haven't had any time to go house hunting."

"Oh, the musical," Josie groaned. "Do you know how it's going? Dad was getting into a real tizzy over it last week." Mr. Grace and the music teacher at his school were staging *Grease*, and rehearsals hadn't been going smoothly.

"I haven't dared to talk to him about it," Mrs. Grace said, smiling. "Whenever I ask, he just throws his hands up in the air. It's bringing out the actor in him—that's for sure."

By now, they'd come to the field in which the

horses were kept. Josie let go of the bridle she was carrying and searched for the handful of carrots in her pocket. Charity was grazing quietly at one edge of the field. Next to her, Hope had stuck her head under the top bar of the rail and post fencing, and was scratching her neck along it.

Josie's heart sank. "Oh, no!" she said anxiously. "Mom! Just look at what Hope's doing. The sweet itch has come back again!"

Her mother groaned, and they both began to hurry toward the horses. As they came closer, they could see that Hope had already rubbed away a large section of her mane, and that she'd bitten sore patches around the dock area at the top of her tail.

"Oh, why did this have to happen now?" Mrs. Grace said in dismay. "The Simmondses are coming to see her right after lessons today. And I thought the insect repellent was working so well!"

Josie hid the bridle behind her back and approached Hope from the front, calling her name softly and holding out some carrots. The horse drew her head out from the fence and gave a low neigh, trotting up to Josie and pushing her muzzle forward to take the tidbit.

Josie's heart melted when she saw her state. "You poor old thing," she said sympathetically, slipping the end of the lead rope over Hope's neck and starting to put on the bridle. "Is that itching driving you crazy?"

"She must have been bitten around dawn," Mrs. Grace said, inspecting the damage. "From now on, we'd better keep her in the stable until later in the morning when the gnats aren't so active. Come on, I'll catch Charity and then let's try and get her cleaned up as much as possible. We can come back for Connie and Tubber later."

"So, who are the Simmondses?" Josie asked, as she and her mother made their way back to the yard. "They don't come for lessons here, do they?"

"No, I've never met them before," Mrs. Grace replied. "Mr. Simmonds called after seeing the newspaper ad. From what I could tell over the phone, he seemed nice enough. He used to ride when he was a child, and they've got a boy of nine who's desperate for a horse of his own. There's a field with stables near their house, and a couple of other horses in it. One's only a yearling, so Hope would have a baby to keep in order."

"She'd like that." Josie smiled, rubbing the horse's nose affectionately. "Well, let's keep our fingers crossed. Who knows, maybe Hope will find her perfect home, too!"

Josie tried hard to get Hope looking her best. She groomed her for ages, arranging the bedraggled mane as nicely as she could over the horse's neck, and polishing her coat with a damp stable cloth until it gleamed. Apart from one patch of spots on her hindquarters and the area around her tail, it was mostly Hope's mane that had been affected; her face, luckily, was clear. Josie could tell Hope was really enjoying all the fuss by the way she put her head in the air and blew gently down her nose when her neck and withers were being brushed.

"Does that make you feel better, poor old itchy thing?" she said, painting some oil on her hooves as a finishing touch.

"What's happened to her mane?" Anna gasped, putting her head over the stable door and gazing at Hope in horror. "It looks awful!"

"Oh, thanks, Anna. Tactful as usual," Josie said, throwing a handful of straw at her. "Some people are coming to look at her after the lessons are finished and I've just spent hours trying to make her beautiful."

"Oops! Sorry," Anna said. "I've put my foot in it again. Well, they probably won't mind a little bit of sweet itch. She's still dear old Hope underneath, after all."

Josie shook her head, smiling. She was used to Anna's habit of saying just what you didn't want to hear. "Could you start getting Charity ready?" she asked. "I haven't touched her yet, and lessons start in half an hour."

"Okay," Anna said. Then, as Ben appeared behind her, she added, "Come on, little brother, let's work as a team." Anna had been born first by twenty minutes, which she always tried to use to her advantage, telling Ben he should respect his elders.

"Hi, Josie," Ben said. "Hope looks great!"

"Thanks, Ben," she replied, giving him a broad smile. "This is a big day for her. There's a family coming to look her over later on."

"Oh, I'm sure they'll like her," he said. "What does it matter if she's going bald, after all?"

"Ben!" Anna called from the stall next door. "I'm

not meant to be doing this all on my own. Come and help!"

Soon, the stables were much livelier. Jane Ramsay arrived to ride out on Connie, and had a quick cup of tea and a little gossip in the office with Mary Grace before saddling up and clattering out of the yard. Then as it was time for lessons to begin, cars started pulling into the driveway.

"Could I have someone to take Jessica around on Charity, please?" Mrs. Grace said, hurrying over to the stalls. "She's just arrived, and Emily's here for Hope, too. Oh, and Ben, could you be a dear and get Tubber ready? Mary's coming up at eleven for a ride."

Josie and Anna took turns leading beginners around for the next few lessons, and soon Josie began looking anxiously toward the yard to see if the Simmondses' car had arrived. Just as the last lesson was ending, an unfamiliar car drove up.

"Mom! I think they're here," Josie hissed from her lookout post by the tree stump, and Mrs. Grace nodded to show that she'd heard. Anna, whose turn it was on the lead rein, turned to look and gave Josie a thumbs-up sign.

"Just before we finish, John," Mrs. Grace said to the boy who was riding Hope, "could you take her for one last trot around the school?"

Hope had a smart, springy trot, and Josie realized her mother wanted to show it off to the Simmondses. She felt very proud of Hope as she watched her trot along at a snappy pace, her head high and her tail held out behind her. It did look rather messy, but Ben was right—what did that matter? She looked over at the yard to see if Ben was there, but he was nowhere to be seen. Shading her eyes, she gazed around and eventually spotted him out in the field, picking up droppings with a wheelbarrow and spade.

A middle-aged man with thin brown hair and glasses got out of the car, followed by a boy who immediately walked over to the school to watch the horses. Seconds later, a short, anxious-looking woman whom Josie assumed was the boy's mother got out of the front passenger seat. A shrill ringing sounded from her shoulder bag, and she muttered something and took out a cell phone, hanging back to answer it.

"Very nice," said Mrs. Grace back in the ring as

John finished. "Now, if you can both turn in and halt, I'll tell you each a couple of things to remember for next week."

If there *is* a next week, Josie thought to herself. Hope might not be here by then. She had another look at the Simmondses, to see if she could find out what they were like. The man was chatting to his son, and the boy listened with a determined expression on his round, freckled face.

She went over toward them, ready to open the gate and let the horses through when the lesson was over, and gave a smile that she hoped was cheerful and welcoming.

"My mother will be here in a minute," she said. "The lesson's almost over. I'm Josie Grace, by the way."

"Oh, don't worry, we're happy to wait," the man replied. "I'm Bill Simmonds, and this is Luke. My wife's in the middle of a crisis at work, I'm afraid, but I'm sure she'll be over in a minute." He smiled, too, but the boy just stared at Josie and didn't speak. "And which is the horse you're selling?" Mr. Simmonds went on.

"The slightly smaller one that the boy's riding,"

Josie said, pointing Hope out. "Did you see her trotting just now? She's a great trotter."

"But I don't want *that* one," Luke said. "I told you, Dad, I like the other one better. Why can't I have her?"

"Oh, no, Hope is the horse we're looking to find a new home for," Josie said, horrified. It had taken her long enough to get used to the idea of parting with Hope—she wasn't ready to consider letting Charity go yet. "Besides, Hope is the perfect first horse," she went on. "She's wonderful with beginners."

"I'm not a beginner," said Luke rudely. "I've had five lessons."

"Now then, Luke," said his father mildly. "Five lessons aren't really enough to teach you all you need to know. It takes a long time to learn how to ride. I think you should listen to what Josie has to say. Why don't you take a ride on Hope? That would give you a better idea of what she's like."

By now, Mrs. Grace had stopped talking to her students, and they were making their way over to the gate. Anna was still holding Charity on the lead rein.

"Anna, could you help Sophie dismount in the

yard, please, and then take Charity back to her stall?" Mrs. Grace called. "John, you can hop off Hope here, if you wouldn't mind." She smiled and waved at the Simmondses, hurrying over to say hello. "I'll be right back," she said, shaking hands with Mr. Simmonds. "I just need a word with John and Sophie's mother about next week. My daughter, Josie, can introduce you to Hope."

"But I told you, I don't want her," Luke grumbled to his father. John, who had jumped down and was giving Hope a pat, stared at him in surprise. "*That's* the one I want," Luke went on, pointing after Charity as she went through the gate and over to the yard. Anna carried on walking, raising her eyebrows at Josie as she passed by. It was pretty clear what she thought of Luke Simmonds.

"But Hope's lovely," John said earnestly. "She tries really hard, and she does just what you tell her to."

Good for you! Josie said to herself, smiling at him. She'd always liked John Butcher, but now she decided he was even nicer than she'd thought. "Bye, Josie," he said, handing her the reins and going off to join his mother and sister in the yard. "See you next week."

"Why don't you have a ride? Then you'd see what John means," Josie suggested to Luke, taking the reins and looping them over Hope's head. She patted the horse's neck, damp with sweat from all her hard work during the lesson. "Come down with me, and I'll take her over to the mounting block."

"All right," Luke said gracelessly, sticking his hands in his pockets.

"How long have you had Hope?" Mr. Simmonds asked as they walked down to the yard. "And why are you selling her?"

"We've had her for nine years," Josie replied. "My mom bought her when Hope was five. The stables and land are about to be sold, so that's why we've got to find a new home for her. She's very gentle and affectionate—she'll nuzzle and groom anyone who'll let her."

Mrs. Grace waved good-bye to the Butchers and came over to join them at the mounting block. "Sorry about that," she said, a little breathlessly. "There seems to be quite a lot to sort out at the moment. Now, are you going to have a ride on Hope?"

"I suppose so," said Luke, grabbing Hope's saddle without any warning and sticking his foot into the stirrup so roughly that he prodded her in the side.

"Wait just a minute!" Mrs. Grace said quickly. "You're facing the wrong way, and you've got the wrong foot in the stirrup, too. You'll end up backward in the saddle if you get on like that! Here, take the reins in your left hand and stand facing her tail. Then put your *left* foot in the stirrup. That's it!"

"Ugh!" said Luke suddenly, dropping the reins which Josie had looped back over Hope's neck. "What's the matter with her mane? Half of it's fallen out, and she's got spots everywhere!"

"Oh, yes," said Mrs. Grace. "I was going to mention that Hope can get sweet itch in the summer. It's a reaction to gnat bites. She doesn't suffer from it too badly and you can ride her without any problem, but sometime she rubs patches away in her mane and tail when she scratches. There's a liquid we put on her to help, and we're going to start keeping her in overnight."

Luke was rubbing his hand against his jeans. "I'm not touching her! I might catch something," he said.

"Now, just a minute—" Mr. Simmonds began, but he was interrupted by his wife, who had finally finished her phone call and was walking over from the car.

She took a brief look at Hope and then said brusquely to Mrs. Grace, "I'm sorry, but we're going to have to leave. I need to get back to the office right away."

"Oh, Mom!" Luke protested. "There's this other horse here—"

His mother cut him off quickly. "We're just wasting time," she said to her husband. "It's perfectly obvious there's something wrong with this horse, and I don't know why you're even bothering to discuss this, Bill. Besides, she's very plain."

Josie drew her breath in sharply and felt herself going red with anger. How dare this horrible woman insult her lovely Hope! Instinctively, she stood closer to her and put an arm around the horse's neck.

"But you can tell she's got a sweet nature, darling," protested Mr. Simmonds, flushing and looking embarrassed. "She might be just the thing for Luke—at least he could try her out."

"I have to get back to the station in time to catch the next train into London," his wife told him sharply. "I don't know why you insist on wasting all our time. This horse is obviously not right for Luke. I don't care how good-natured she is; she looks awful, and we're not taking her. That's all there is to it."

Mrs. Grace had had enough. "You're absolutely right," she said, drawing herself up and standing very straight. "There's no point in discussing this further. Your son would be very lucky to have a horse with such a perfect temperament as this, but I wouldn't dream of letting you buy her. There are plenty of people around who know about horses and would never judge Hope at face value, like you just have."

"Oh, there are, are there?" said Mrs. Simmonds, with a brittle smile on her face. "Well, I hope you find one of them to take her off your hands. Good luck—you'll need it!" And she turned and marched back to the car, followed by her sheepish-looking husband and sulky son.

"Way to go, Mom!" Josie told her mother as they

watched them go. "Why did she have to be so rude?" She laid her head against the horse's neck, glad her good, kind Hope couldn't understand the insults that had been thrown at her.

CHAPTER FOUR

"I thought the boy was bad enough," Anna said as she walked up the path to the house with Josie and Ben, "but it sounds like his mother was even worse."

"Oh, she was awful!" Josie told them. "She was so rude about Hope—you should have heard her! All she wanted to do was get back to her stupid office."

"Well, Hope's had a lucky escape, then," Ben said. "I wonder what your dad's made for lunch, Josie? I'm starving!" Robert Grace was a wonderful cook, and Josie's mom was more than happy to leave the family meals up to him.

"I wouldn't expect too much," Josie replied. "He's so busy with this musical they're putting on at his school he hardly goes near the kitchen these days. They're doing a version of *Grease*—you know, that rock-and-roll musical. John Travolta was in the film."

Her father taught at a different school from the one they all went to—much to Josie's relief. There would have been no escaping the musical otherwise, at home or at school.

By now, they were nearly at the front door to School Farm. "What on earth is he doing?" Anna exclaimed, peering through the leaded windows into the sitting room. "Get out the straitjacket, Josie—I think your father's gone mad!"

Ben and Josie crowded around behind her, and they all looked through, to see Mr. Grace leaping around the room like a maniac, blond hair falling over his face as he twirled and twisted. "Oh, he's dancing," Josie groaned. "Don't look—it's too embarrassing!"

"He's actually not that bad," Anna said, cupping her hand on the glass to cut down the reflection. "Not exactly John Travolta, but quite good for an old-timer. Oh, he's gone down on his knees—could be tricky! Can he get himself back up again? Yes!

He's done it. Whoops, straight into the bookcase. Just when it was all going so well . . ."

"All right, Anna!" Josie said, laughing and dragging her away from the window. "We don't need a running commentary, thanks very much."

They opened the front door, and the strains of "Summer Lovin'" came drifting out on the air. "If I hear that song one more time, I'm going to scream," Josie said, looking through the sitting room door to see her father sitting on a chair, cradling his knee in both hands.

"Great!" he said enthusiastically as he caught sight of them. "Just in time! I need two volunteers to try out these new dance steps. Ben and Anna, you'll do."

"Oh, no! He's my brother," Anna said, pulling away. "I don't want to touch him!"

"All right then, Josie and Ben," Mr. Grace said, arranging them both in position with Ben standing back to back with Josie and holding her right arm up with his left.

"I'll watch and criticize," Anna offered, perching on the sofa. "That's what I'm best at, after all."

Soon, though, Anna was laughing too hard to

speak. Josie managed to follow her father's instructions, but Ben seemed to have two left feet and he was always forgetting which way he was meant to turn.

"All right," Mr. Grace sighed, after Ben had gone lumbering off in the wrong direction yet again, leaving Josie holding on to thin air, "maybe we should call it a day."

"I don't think I could take much more." Anna gasped, holding her stomach. "I haven't laughed so much in ages!"

"Well, let's see how good *you* are," Ben said, pulling his sister to her feet and spinning her off around the room. "Now we can all enjoy ourselves at your expense!"

"Enough! Enough!" shouted Mr. Grace, as Anna's flailing arms toppled a lamp and threatened to knock over a vase. "Time for lunch, I think."

"Thank goodness, that's over," Josie said, heading for the door. "Mom's coming in a minute. She's just making a couple of phone calls in the office."

"No, I've finished and I'm here," Mary Grace said, looking into the room from the hallway.

"What's going on? Sounds like you've been having a party!"

"You don't want to know," her husband said, putting an arm around her shoulder and taking her off to the kitchen. "Come and have some lunch and tell me about these people who came to see Hope."

"They were horrible," Josie said, following her parents down the hall, with Ben and Anna close behind. "The boy was really spoiled and the mother was unbelievable!"

"It *is* the very worst time for Hope to have sweet itch," Mrs. Grace said anxiously. "I've just been on the phone with the vet about it. That new lotion we've got just doesn't seem to be working." She sat down at the kitchen table, which was covered with plates of salad, ham, and salami, different kinds of cheese and crusty bread. "Oh, Rob, this looks great. Thanks for getting it all ready."

"You'd think people would realize sweet itch is just a temporary thing, though," Josie said, pinching a tomato and popping it into her mouth. "And it doesn't affect the way Hope behaves."

"Yes, but, unfortunately, first impressions matter," her mother replied. She picked up a slice of cucumber and crunched on it absentmindedly. "I'm getting more worried about where Hope's going to go," she admitted, looking up at Josie. "There's no one else lined up to see her, and we haven't had any phone calls about the ad for a couple of days."

"Oh, well, something'll turn up," Josie said, rattling around in the cutlery drawer for knives and forks to lay on the table. "Remember, it took the Atterburys a while to get in touch with us about Faith."

"I know," Mrs. Grace said carefully, "but just in case, I've also been on the phone to Mrs. Peabody. At the animal sanctuary."

"The animal sanctuary?" Josie said, pausing with a serving spoon in midair. Ben and Anna glanced up from their seats at the table, too. They looked as shocked as Josie felt.

"Only as a last resort," her mother said. "I think it would be a good idea for us to have something up our sleeve if we can't find Hope a home anywhere else. She'd have lots of company, and Mrs. Peabody looks after those animals really well."

"But isn't the sanctuary for animals who've been mistreated?" Anna asked.

"Not necessarily," Mrs. Grace replied. "They also take in pets whose owners can't keep them anymore, for one reason or another. I've arranged to go and see her on Monday afternoon. Why don't you come along and have a look, too? We can go after school. It might be interesting."

"Okay," Josie said mechanically. She sat down at the table, but her appetite seemed to have vanished. Hope at the animal sanctuary? Something about the thought made her feel terribly sad. They'd loved and looked after Hope for years—if they took her to the sanctuary, it would feel like they were abandoning her. Like they didn't care anymore.

A tall, plump woman with an exploding bun of wispy gray hair came out from behind a counter in the small shop at the entrance to the Peabody Animal Welfare Sanctuary. "Great to see you!" she beamed at Josie and her mother, shaking their hands. "Welcome to PAWS! Of course, I suppose we should be known as Paws and Hooves! Or, strictly speaking, Paws, Hooves, and Claws," she added, beginning to look rather flustered, "as we have birds, too. And there is actually a snake at the moment, though I don't know where he'd fit in. Anyway," she finished with some relief, "I'm Elizabeth Peabody, and I'm delighted to meet you."

"Mary Grace," smiled Josie's mother, "and this is my daughter, Josie. Thanks so much for letting us take a look around."

"Not at all," said Mrs. Peabody, turning the sign on the door to the CLOSED side and locking it. "Only too glad to help. Your horse sounds lovely, and I do hope you'll manage to find a family to take her—but if you don't, I think we might be able to squeeze her in here."

"Thank you very much for the offer," said Josie dutifully. She'd been coached by her mother in the car about looking grateful and appreciating what Mrs. Peabody was prepared to do for them. "It's very kind of you to—" Then she couldn't help letting out a scream, and clapping her hand over her mouth. There was something moving in Mrs. Peabody's bosom! She could just see the top of a small, black, scrawny *thing*, wriggling around.

"Josie! What *is* the matter with you?" said her mother, horrified, as Josie pointed wordlessly toward whatever it was.

"Oh, this!" said Mrs. Peabody, fishing down inside her shirt. She came out with her hand closed gently around something, and opened her fingers slowly for Josie to see. A tiny baby bat, only about three inches long, flopped around on her palm. "I'm keeping him warm," she said softly. "Someone found him in a garage and brought him in yesterday. We're feeding him milk with an eyedropper."

"He's so small!" Josie managed to say now that she had gotten over the initial shock.

"He is, indeed," said Mrs. Peabody, popping him back down her front. "When he's a bit stronger, we're going to see how he does when he tries to fly, but this is the best place for him at the moment. Now, come and meet the others."

Josie decided she did like Mrs. Peabody, after all. They followed her through the back of the shop and into a small courtyard with wire cages all around. "Birds on this side," she announced with a wave of her arm that Josie was frightened would send the bat into orbit sooner than planned. "Rabbits and guinea pigs over here, and we even have a badger at the moment, though we're hoping to release him back in the wild very soon."

"Where's all the noise coming from?" Josie asked, as yaps and howls rose in the air.

"Come this way and I'll show you," said Mrs. Peabody, leading them toward a doorway in the far wall of the courtyard. They went through it to find a long, low building, with fencing all along one side. About twenty dogs of various shapes and sizes were pressed up against the wire, wagging their tails and barking eagerly at the visitors.

"Do you try to find homes for them?" Josie asked, her hands over her ears. She couldn't bear the thought of all these creatures, desperate for company and attention, living here.

"Well, some of them can be adopted," said Mrs. Peabody, "but others just aren't suitable as family pets, unfortunately. If they're nervous already, the way they've been treated can make them aggressive toward people. You wouldn't believe the injuries I've seen. Cigarette burns, rope marks, scalds from boiling water—we've had them all."

"Oh, how awful!" Josie said, looking at her in distress. "How could people do things like that to animals? What have they ever done to hurt anyone?"

"It's very upsetting," Mrs. Peabody agreed. "Still, we do our best for them once they've arrived here. Now, I expect you'd like to see our horses and donkeys, wouldn't you?" She led them on past a large shed that had a sign, THE REPTILE HOUSE!, and out to a field, which sloped downhill. There were about ten donkeys in it, and two horses grazing near the fence.

"I won't try and name all the donkeys," Mrs. Peabody said, "but the chestnut horse is called Hercules, and the dun horse we've named Sally. We found her in the water, trapped in a river."

"What happened to her legs?" asked Mrs. Grace, looking at the nasty scars all over them.

"We think she must have torn them on some barbed wire," Mrs. Peabody said. "That's why she'd fallen in the river. She was lucky not to get tetanus. The wounds are healing up now, but I don't think the hair will ever grow back."

"And what about Hercules? Where's he from?" Josie asked, watching the big chestnut. He lifted his head and returned her gaze with big, sad eyes, then went back to eating the grass.

"Someone found him in the basement of an

abandoned house in the city," Mrs. Peabody answered. "From what we can make out, he was going to be part of some plan to offer carriage rides that went wrong, and he was just abandoned to starve to death. He nearly did, too. Here, boy! Come on, Hercules!" She whistled, and the horse came walking slowly and hesitantly over to them, his head held low.

Josie held out her hand, and Hercules sniffed it suspiciously. "Can I give him a mint?" she asked.

"He'd like that," said Mrs. Peabody, patting Hercules' neck. "After all, he deserves a bit of spoiling. Just be careful when you hold it out to him—he's head shy. Someone's obviously beaten him around the face at some time in his life."

Mrs. Grace shook her head sadly while Josie cautiously held out the mint on her palm. "You poor old thing," she whispered, as Hercules snatched it up and crunched it between his teeth. "How could anyone do that to you? I'm so sorry."

But the horse just flicked back his ears and wandered away.

"We had to have our other resident horse put down a couple of weeks ago," Mrs. Peabody said, "so we do have room for one more at the moment. If you're interested, you should let me know quickly. I could get a phone call at any time, and that place would be gone."

"Thanks very much," said Mrs. Grace, with a look at Josie's downcast face. "We'll give you a call just as soon as we can."

"Mrs. Peabody's quite a character, isn't she?" Mrs. Grace said as they drove away from the sanctuary. "You can tell she loves the animals, though. It's good to think of some creature that's been badly treated getting a second chance with her."

"Oh, sure," Josie agreed. "For a horse like Hercules, it must be great to end up there. But our Hope? Come on, Mom—she's not that old, and she hasn't been abused or anything. She's been a part of our family for most of her life. The sanctuary's just not the right place for her—it really isn't!"

Mrs. Grace gazed at the road ahead and didn't speak for a while. "Look," she said eventually, "I do think we ought to have some plan in mind for Hope in case nothing else turns up. Let's face it—time's running out and we've got to be realistic. I think we should consider Mrs. Peabody's offer very seriously, Josie. I don't want to lose what might turn out to be Hope's only chance by dragging our feet about it."

Josie wasn't sure at first quite how to reply, but she knew better than to risk a head-on clash with her mother. Once Mrs. Grace made her mind up, she wouldn't budge, and Josie didn't want to push her into a decision. "Today's Monday," Josie said. "Why don't we wait until this weekend? If nothing else has turned up during the week, we can talk to Mrs. Peabody again. What do you think about that?"

"Okay, then," said her mother. "But I'd say Friday at the latest. If there are no other offers by then, we go for the sanctuary."

CHAPTER FIVE

"Come on, Josie," Anna said as they walked down the road toward the village. "We're supposed to be doing this project together. At least you could help me decide which explorer to choose!"

"Did any of them go on horseback?" Josie asked.

"Well, I suppose the ones who went overland," Anna replied, with a touch of impatience. "They couldn't exactly hop on a train, could they? But you don't have to bring horses into *everything*, Josie. Couldn't you think about something else for a while?"

"Oh, I suppose so," Josie said, as they turned off Northgate's main street and started down a narrow street on the edge of the village. "I'm just so worried about Hope, it's hard to concentrate on anything else." She'd told Anna all about their visit to the animal sanctuary the day before, and her mother's deadline. "Don't you feel the same?" she added.

"I know what you mean," Anna replied, serious for once. "But I don't see what we can do about it. Worrying isn't going to get us anywhere. Why don't you think about this geography project instead? It might take your mind off things. And Ben's playing soccer at school, so the computer's free for a while." She stopped at her front door, then pushed it open.

"Hello, there," said Lynne Marshall, the twins' mother, who was sitting in a chair by the window with a huge book of paint swatches on her lap. "Josie, I haven't seen you in a while. How are you?"

"Oh, fine, thanks, Lynne," said Josie. She knew how much Anna's mom disliked being called Mrs. Marshall, especially since she and her husband had separated. It was true—she hadn't been to Ben and Anna's house for a long time, and now she realized how much she had missed her visits. She'd been so involved in everything that was happening at the stables lately, there hadn't been time for much else.

The house was very nice. It might have been

small, but Lynne arranged everything so beautifully that it always felt cozy and welcoming. She was a trained artist, though these days she worked mainly as a painter and decorator, and she had filled the house with light and color. In winter there was almost always a fire burning in the open grate when Anna and Ben got back from school. On sunny days, the French windows looking out on to the paved courtyard at the back of the house were thrown open. Today, the scent of honeysuckle floated in, and a bumblebee buzzed around a pot of white lilies.

Josie looked round the peppermint green walls of the sitting room. "Something's different in here," she said. "What is it?"

"Aha!" Lynne replied with a grin. "See if you can figure it out." She had short blond hair and blue eyes, and looked so unlike Ben and Anna. They got their dark coloring from their father's side of the family.

"Got it!" said Josie after a couple of minutes. "That's a different painting over the fireplace, isn't it?" She gazed at the bright, swirling landscape. "Is it one you've just done?"

"I wish," said Lynne, getting up and casting a

critical eye over at the picture. "It's been gathering dust in the studio for the past five years. I felt like a change, that's all."

"I like it, Mom. Those poppies are wonderful," Anna said. "I always love your flowers. You should do a few more like that and see if your agent could fix up another exhibition."

"And when am I going to get the chance to do any more painting?" Lynne said as she went back to her chair. "I'm worn out with all this decorating work, and there's no time for anything else."

"Give it up, then," Anna suggested. "Just paint for a while."

"And what would we live on? Fresh air?" came the reply. "At least the business brings some regular money in. Painting's going to have to wait for a while, I'm afraid. Now, can I fix you both a sandwich?"

"No thanks, Mom," Anna said. "We're going to do some work on the computer." She took Josie's arm and steered her toward the study on the other side of the staircase. "Come on," she said. "I've decided for us. We're going to write about Mary Kingsley—she's the only female explorer I could find. She paddled up the Congo in a dugout canoe. How about that for girl power?"

An hour later, Anna pushed the computer keyboard back across the desk and rolled her stiff shoulders around in a circle. "Well, I think that's covered everything," she said. "I'll just print out what we've typed and we can copy the maps at school tomorrow."

"You were right, Anna," Josie admitted, cutting out the picture of Mary Kingsley they'd downloaded and were planning to put on the cover of their project. "It's been good for me to think about something different for a change. And I never realized how useful the Internet is." Anna and Ben had been really excited when they got the computer as a birthday present from their father, but it was the first time that Josie had taken an interest in it.

"It's great, isn't it?" Anna agreed. "And it's done wonders for our project."

"Wait a minute!" Josie said suddenly, putting down the scissors and looking excitedly at Anna. "Why don't we see if there's anything about sweet itch on the Internet? Mom says she's tried everything for Hope, but maybe there's some new treatment she hasn't heard of!"

"That's not a bad idea," Anna said, catching her enthusiasm. "Hang on, I'll just get connected again and give it a go."

In a few seconds, she was hooked back on to the Internet. Josie pulled up her chair, looking eagerly at the screen as Anna typed in the words "sweet itch" and clicked on the FIND button.

"Got it!" she said a minute or so later. "Josie, you're brilliant! There's a whole Web site just for sweet itch." Together they waited for the site to be opened, and then, as if by magic, the latest information began to appear.

"This is amazing!" Josie said, reaching for a pad of paper. "We'd better make some notes—there's so much to take in!"

They scrolled down the screen, copying down any remedies that seemed effective. There were extracts from scientific journals and photos of horses suffering from the complaint, which made them both wince. "At least Hope doesn't look as bad as some of these poor horses," Josie said. What she found most exciting, though, were the firsthand reports from people who'd tried out the various cures on their own animals.

"This person says castor oil's good for helping the hair grow back," Anna said. "Have you seen that? Halfway down the page?"

"Hang on," Josie said, scribbling furiously, "I'm still copying this part about the cream and zinc oxide powder." She looked back at the screen, then let out a yelp as her eye caught sight of an entry near the bottom. "Anna!" she said, grabbing her arm as she read on. "There's a woman who's developed a spray that's meant to be ninety-eight percent effective. She's used it with her own horses, and now she's looking for people to test it out—for free! Here, read it for yourself."

Anna ran her eyes over the words flickering in front of them and turned to smile at Josie. "Bingo!" she said. "Let's send her a message right now! After all, what have we got to lose?" She clicked on the e-mail address and began to type.

"This spray couldn't be dangerous, could it?" Josie asked, getting cold feet all of a sudden. "What if it makes Hope worse?"

"I don't think that's likely," Anna replied

confidently. "It seems to have been thought out very scientifically. Anyway, if it shows any signs of harming her, we can just stop using it. Oh, Josie, maybe this will really help Hope. We've got to give it a try!"

At that moment, Lynne Marshall's voice came through the open door. "You haven't been on the Internet all this time, have you?" she said, poking her head in. "For goodness' sake, Anna, remember the phone bill! I'm not made of money, you know."

"No, we've only just gone back on, Mom," Anna replied, turning from the desk to face her. "Josie just had this brainstorm about finding out if there's anything—"

"Well, whatever it is, do it as quickly as possible, please," her mother said sharply, and went back out of the room.

Anna sighed as she continued typing the message, finally showing it to Josie for approval.

"That looks fine," Josie said. "Thanks! It might not work but, like you say, what have we got to lose?" Then she took another look at Anna's gloomy face and added, "Is anything wrong? You were really excited a second ago."

"Oh, I'm just worried about Mom," Anna replied. "She gets grumpy out of the blue and she's tired most of the time—I think she's working too hard. It's tough, all that stripping wallpaper and sanding and painting. You should see the muscles in her arms."

"Maybe she needs another evening out with my mom," Josie suggested, after thinking for a while. "You and Ben could always stay overnight at our house."

"Yes, she'd like that," Anna replied. "They get along really well, don't they?"

"Just like we do," Josie said, giving her friend a quick hug. She felt guilty: Anna had problems of her own, and she hadn't even noticed. "Look," she said, "why don't we have that sandwich now and then take the horses out for a ride? There's still plenty of time before it gets dark, and I feel like some fresh air after all this work. What do you say?"

"Good idea!" Anna replied, jumping up. "I'll just get changed, and then we can grab something to eat."

So, after a peanut-butter-and-jelly sandwich and a lecture from Lynne about rules for going on the

Internet ("after six o'clock and for half an hour at the most"), Josie put the notes they'd taken into her schoolbag, and the two of them began to walk back to the stables. Mrs. Grace was busy polishing a saddle in the tack room when they arrived.

"Mom!" Josie said, bursting in. "We've found out all sorts of information on the Internet about sweet itch. Look, I've made loads of notes! And we've contacted someone who's developed a new spray and wants people to test it out. Anna's asked for it to be sent here!"

"I'm a bit doubtful about miracle cures," Mrs. Grace said, scanning the pages Josie had given her. "In my experience, they don't often do much good. Still, thanks for taking all this trouble. I hadn't heard of using castor oil on the scars, but let's give it a try!"

"Can we take the horses out for a quick ride, Mom?" Josie asked, reaching for a couple of bridles.

"Just so long as you're back before dinner," Mrs. Grace said. "We've got to have Hope safely in the stable before those gnats start biting."

"We won't go for long," Anna replied. "I'll get the horses while you get out of your school gear," she said, taking the bridles from Josie.

"Bring them in one at a time," Mrs. Grace called after them. "You can't handle them both at once, Anna!"

"So, where shall we go?" Josie said as they turned out of the stables. It felt great to be on horseback after spending so much time in front of the computer. Charity began to pull, eager to be off, so Josie shortened the reins, patted the horse's neck, and spoke quietly to calm her down.

"Why don't we go through the village and then up Baker's Hill and back through the fields?" Anna replied, falling in behind her on Hope. "Ben said he had a great ride with Tubber there the other day, and it won't take too long."

"Fine," Josie said, turning on to the road and back toward the village. "Oh, Charity, stop doing that!" The horse was beginning to take little steps backward, making a fuss about a piece of plastic flapping in the hedge. Josie squeezed her outside leg behind the girth to stop Charity's hindquarters from swinging out into the road and soon got her walking. "I think she's been having too much of that young grass," she said, turning back to smile at Anna.

"We'll have to keep her in overnight with Hope."

The horses' shoes struck the pavement as they trotted along the road, quiet now without any traffic. Josie felt her spirits rise as they went. It was good to be out in the open with Anna. She took another quick glance behind, and Anna gave her a thumbs-up sign. Hope's poor bedraggled mane and sparse tail weren't looking any better, but Josie told herself that she and Anna were going to help her get over the sweet itch, if it was the last thing they did. One of the cures they'd read about was bound to work, even if the spray didn't turn out to be a miracle. And someone would offer Hope a home, she was sure of it. She'd have another word with a few of the students who came to the stables.

Then she looked forward again, and groaned. Hanging around by the bus shelter were Mark Lee, a big bully in the year above them at school, and a fair-haired boy in a leather jacket she hadn't come across before. They were sitting on mountain bikes, watching as Josie and Anna approached, obviously bored and looking for trouble.

"Try to ignore them," Anna called softly behind her, and Josie tried to relax. She didn't want Charity to sense her tension—she was high-spirited enough this afternoon as it was.

"Well, what have we got here?" Mark sneered as they came closer, narrowing his eyes and staring at them. "Two little girlies out for a ride. How sweet!"

"Look at the ugly one!" crowed his friend, as Anna rode past on Hope. "What's the matter with her? Looks like all her hair's dropping out. Couldn't you find a better horse to ride than that old nag?"

Josie bit her lip, furious but determined not to lose her temper. Anna, though, had forgotten her own advice about staying calm. "She's got a horse version of acne," Josie heard her say sweetly. "Something you'd know all about. Maybe there's a good cream you could recommend?"

Josie looked back and saw the boy's spotty face flush a deep red. Oh no! she thought to herself. Anna, that's not going to do any good!

"Very funny," he said, riding his bike out into the road behind them. "Think that's clever, do you? You're out of your league here, Miss Stuck-up Princess. Come on Mark, let's have some fun!"

They rode along some distance behind the two horses, circling their bikes from one side of the road to the other, whistling, and shouting. Charity put her ears back and her tail began to swish angrily. She snorted a couple of times, but Josie didn't dare turn around and tell the boys to get lost.

Then, disaster struck. Either Mark or his friend—she couldn't tell which of the two it was—suddenly let out a piercing blast on a horn. With a squeal of fear, Charity reared up in panic, throwing her forelegs frantically out in midair.

"Josie!" she heard Anna scream, as she desperately fought to keep control of the terrified horse.

CHAPTER SIX

Josie tried to sit as deep in the saddle as she could, to tell Charity that she was still there and still in charge. She was relieved that, after her first terrified lunge, the horse had stopped rearing. But her ears were right back and she was obviously very nervous. What frightened Josie most of all was the thought that if Charity bolted straight through the village, they'd come out on to a busy main road, where the traffic thundered along at all times of the day and night. She kept a tight hold on the reins, but Charity was throwing her head around and dancing all over the road with jumpy little steps.

Thinking quickly, Josie tried to turn her around in a circle, so that even if she did take off, she'd be galloping away from the main road. Unfortunately, that meant she was facing the boys, who were still shouting and laughing behind them, but she felt it was the safest option. She patted Charity's neck and spoke soft reassuring words to her, but the horse was spooked and wasn't going to be calmed down easily.

"Charity! It's okay," called Anna, trotting toward her on Hope. She brought the calm, steady mare up to stand beside her daughter. "Look!" she said soothingly. "Hope's not frightened. She knows they can't do you any harm."

"Oh, can't we?" shouted the boy in the leather jacket. "Do you want some more of this?" And he put his hand threateningly on the big black horn fixed to his handlebars. "Doesn't like that, does she?" he jeered.

Don't blow that again! Josie thought to herself. She knew that if there was another blast, she'd have no hope of keeping Charity under control. How could that stupid boy be so thoughtless? Didn't he realize the danger he was putting her in?

"Don't be such a fool!" Anna shouted at him. "Somebody could get hurt!"

"Well, it won't be me," he sneered, "so what do I care?"

"Oh, won't it?" Anna muttered under her breath. She shortened her reins, as though about to move off.

"Anna, don't go!" Josie said urgently. "Hope's the only thing that's stopping Charity from bolting. Please, stay with me!" As soon as Hope had walked up to them, Josie had felt some of the tension leave her horse. Hope seemed to sense how frightened Charity was and stood squarely between her and the boys, shielding her from their shouts and blocking her way as if to prevent her from bolting. Without Hope's reassuring presence, Josie didn't know what might happen.

"Come on, Steve," said Mark Lee uneasily. "Give it a break now. Let's go back to my place and watch TV."

He turned his bike around and began to pedal back down the road. With one last defiant gesture to Josie and Anna, the other boy followed him. "We'll be waiting for you another time!" he called over his shoulder.

"Oh, will you?" Anna said grimly. "Big coward! I'm a match for you any day of the week."

Josie let out a long, shaky breath. She knew now

that Charity wasn't going to gallop off—the horse's breathing was steadier and her ears were flicking back and forth as she watched the danger going farther and farther away. She obviously felt safer standing next to her mother.

"Hope's amazing!" she said to Anna, her voice quivering. "I think she must be the bravest, calmest horse in the world. Charity was about to bolt, I know she was."

Anna patted Hope and then slipped her feet out of the stirrups and jumped off, looping the reins over her neck. She stood by Charity's head, rubbing her nose and speaking softly to her. "You can tell by her eyes she's still scared," she said. "I think we should go back, don't you? What if I lead Hope and walk next to Charity? Then I can take hold of her if anything goes wrong or we run into those morons again."

"Thanks, Anna," Josie said gratefully. "I'm just so glad Hope was here. I don't know what I'd have done without her."

"She's one in a million, isn't she?" Anna replied, kissing the horse's neck.

"It makes me so angry when people are horrible

about the way she looks," Josie went on. "Why can't they see how special she is underneath? I can't bear to think of Hope going to the sanctuary, I just can't!"

However, inquiries from people interested in buying Hope seemed to have entirely dried up. Josie asked her mother anxiously on Wednesday whether anyone else had called, but Mrs. Grace just shook her head. Josie was finding it hard to keep feeling positive. She had to admit that Hope's chances of finding a new home in the next few days seemed slim. Then, just as she was bringing her in from the field to spend the night in the stable, she heard the phone ring in the office, where her mother happened to be working.

"Who do you think that is, Hope?" she said as she cleaned out the horse's feet with a hoof pick, checking to see if she had picked up any stones. "Could it be someone asking about you?"

She called in at the office when she'd finished filling the water bucket and putting some more straw in the stall. "That wasn't a call about Hope, was it?" she asked her mother. "I heard the phone ring about ten minutes ago."

"Well, as a matter of fact it was," Mrs. Grace said, pushing back her chair.

"And?" Josie asked eagerly. "Come on, Mom, don't keep me in suspense!"

"I'm afraid it wasn't a serious offer," her mother replied. "Some children who are friends of John and Sophie—you know, the Butchers—called to see if we'd sold Hope yet. They want a horse more than anything else, and John had told them all about her."

"So what's the catch?" Josie said.

"They live in a block of apartments," her mother replied with a smile, "and they wanted to keep Hope in the elevator. She's so laid-back she'd probably think that was just fine, but I don't really think it's an option, do you?"

"No, I suppose not," Josie sighed, slumping in a chair on the other side of the desk.

"Cheer up, dear," her mother said gently. "If Hope does have to go to the sanctuary, she'll probably be perfectly happy there, and we could go to visit her whenever we wanted. There are worse places she could end up."

"Maybe you're right," Josie said dispiritedly. "I've

worried about this so much I can't seem to think straight anymore."

"Hello, you two," said Robert Grace, appearing at the office door with a bulging case and an armful of textbooks. "Everything okay?"

Josie looked at him for a moment without speaking. Her face must have shown how dejected she was feeling, because he dumped the books he was carrying on the desk and drew up a chair next to her. "What's all this doom and gloom, then?" he asked gently. "Come on, if anyone's depressed, it should be me. I've just had a truly terrible rehearsal. Sandy doesn't know her lines, Danny's lost his voice, and there's only just over a week to go. Beat that for worries!"

"It's Hope," Josie said. "We can't seem to find anyone who wants her."

"Okay, you win," said Mr. Grace immediately, and Josie couldn't help smiling. Her father had a knack of cheering her up.

"I have told Josie, though, that I think the animal sanctuary isn't such a bad idea," said Mrs. Grace, closing her accounts book. "I'm sure Hope would be well looked after there."

"And it might only be for a little while," Mr.

Grace suggested. "After all, we could still look for a family to take Hope while she stayed at the sanctuary, couldn't we?"

"I guess so," Josie said, leaning back in her chair and pushing her feet against the desk. "It's just so unsettling, not knowing what's going to happen to her and whether she'll be gone in a few days or not."

"I agree with you there," said her mother with feeling. "I'm not sure whether to take any bookings for next week, or how much more feed to order. Everything seems to be up in the air. We don't even know where we're going to be living in a couple of months!"

"Look," said Mr. Grace, "this is a difficult time for all of us to get through—nobody can deny that. We'll just have to take it step by step and tackle the problems one at a time. At least Hope has somewhere to go, even if the sanctuary isn't perfect, and who knows—something else might turn up." He looked earnestly at Josie and her mother. "The most important thing is, we've still got each other. If we stick together, we can get through this!"

Josie knew in her heart of hearts her father was right. Besides, moping around wasn't going to do

Hope any good. "You're right!" she said, stretching out a hand to hold each of her parents'. "Things could be better, but they could be a lot worse, too."

"Absolutely, sweet pea," her father smiled. "That's the right way to look at it." Then suddenly he jumped up and announced, "I know what we need— a party! There are a hundred good reasons for throwing one. Well, three at least. We could thank everyone who's come to the stables over the years, and everyone who's helped me with the musical, and cheer ourselves up at the same time! Let's have it the weekend after next, right after *Grease* has finished."

"But will that give us enough time to organize everything?" Mrs. Grace objected. "When there's so much else to be done, do we really need a party, too?"

"Yes, we do!" Josie exclaimed. "I think it's a brilliant idea. Come on, Mom—let's have some fun and try to forget our problems for a while!"

The next day, though, Josie came back from school to a sight that sent all those good resolutions flying out the window. There, parked in the yard, was a van belonging to the Peabody Animal Welfare Sanctuary. Her heart lurched. What was going on?

Hope still had another day's grace, didn't she, before her mother called the sanctuary? Surely, she wouldn't have gone back on their agreement without some warning. . . .

She rushed up the path to School Farm and burst through the front door and down the hall into the kitchen. Her mother and Mrs. Peabody were sitting over mugs of tea at the big pine table.

"It's all right, dear," said Mrs. Grace, holding up a hand as soon as she saw Josie's face. "You don't have to worry—we're not deciding anything. Mrs. Peabody's just came by with quite an interesting proposal."

"For Hope?" Josie said breathlessly, letting her schoolbag drop to the ground.

"That's right," Mrs. Peabody said, smiling. "I was just telling your mother that I had a visit yesterday from a group of physically challenged children. There's a place called Friendship House not far from us—have you heard of it?"

Josie shook her head, joining them at the kitchen table.

"Well, they take physically challenged children for weekends, to give their caretakers a break," Mrs.

Peabody went on. "The place is run by a wonderful young woman called Liz Tallant. She's quite an extraordinary person—full of energy and ideas."

Mrs. Peabody took a sip of her tea and seemed to be lost in thought for a moment.

"And—?" Josie prompted her, almost bursting with impatience. What *was* this interesting proposal? She was dying to find out.

"Oh, yes," Mrs. Peabody said, gathering herself together again. "Well, they've got a couple of donkeys at the center—I've heard it's a very pleasant place, lots of beautiful grounds—and Liz really wants to adopt a horse. She was asking about Sally, but I'm afraid the poor thing's much too nervous to cope with lots of boisterous children."

"Apparently, they need a very steady, gentle horse who doesn't mind noise," Mrs. Grace put in. "Does that ring any bells, Josie?"

"Yes, it does," Josie said slowly. There were a hundred questions buzzing around in her head, but a small, excited feeling was also growing in the pit of her stomach.

"I'm sure there's a lot you need to find out," said Mrs. Peabody, as though she could read her mind.

"If you agree, I'll talk to Liz and she can give you a call and arrange to meet. If she's interested in Hope, that is."

"I think that sounds like a good plan," Mrs. Grace said. "What do you think, Josie?"

"I agree," Josie said, her eyes shining. "Thanks, Mrs. Peabody!"

What Hope enjoyed most of all was being useful, and Josie was sure she'd love to stay active. The donkeys at the center would be company for her, but she'd still get plenty of care and attention. It sounded wonderful. Liz Tallant had to be interested in Hope—she just had to be!

CHAPTER
SEVEN

"What do you think, Josie?" said her mother as they sat in the car outside Friendship House. "It seems like a nice place, doesn't it?"

"It does," Josie agreed, looking at the sprawling, honey-colored stone building in front of them. The original house must have been quite old, but it had obviously been renovated over the years. To one side, a single story extension in the shape of a rectangle with three sides was built around a small lawn. Pots of bright red geraniums were dotted along the driveway and on either side of the front door, and the sound of piano music floated out through an open window.

"It's very peaceful," Josie added, looking around

for signs of life. "I wonder where everyone is?"

"Well, Liz said this was their changeover time," Mrs. Grace said. "She's expecting a new group of children tomorrow, and the last group has just left. That's why she asked us to come today, so we'd have a chance to talk without too many interruptions. Come on, let's get going. We don't want to keep her waiting!"

They rang the bell, and a minute or so later the door was flung open by a slim, brown-haired young woman in a striped T-shirt and jeans. "Hi, there, I'm Liz Tallant," she said, ushering them in with a broad smile that lit up her face. "I'm so glad you could come! Let's go straight to my office and we can talk."

She led the way into a pleasant-looking room near the front entrance. There was a large desk by the window, and several armchairs and a sofa along one wall. "Have a seat," Liz said, settling into one of the armchairs herself.

"We'll try not to take up too much of your time," Mrs. Grace said politely as she and Josie sat down. "I'm sure you must have plenty to do."

"Oh, you shouldn't worry about that!" Liz

replied warmly. "It's great to meet you, and I can't wait to hear all about your horse. But let me tell you a bit about Friendship House first, so you can see if you think it might be the right place for her."

Josie took the other chair and gazed around the office while her mother and Liz talked. There was so much to look at! Paintings, drawings, and cards were hung over every inch of the walls, and a huge cork bulletin board was covered in photographs. She could see children at the beach, in a swimming pool, covered in mud, cooking, painting—all of them looking busy and really happy.

"We take physically challenged children, to stay for a week or two at a time," Liz was saying. "We try to make it as much fun as we can, and it's also a break for the children's caretakers. Looking after them can be a twenty-four-hour job, and everyone needs some time off, don't they?"

She jumped up, saying, "Look, why don't I take you around, so you can get more of an idea of the place?"

Josie got the feeling Liz was much happier doing something than sitting still and talking. She seemed to radiate energy and enthusiasm as she showed them into a big, airy room with lots of comfortable armchairs and a few low tables arranged in groups around it. The music Josie had heard when they'd first arrived was coming from a CD player in the corner, and it gave the place a lovely tranquil feeling. She looked around, imagining the room full of life and activity.

"This is our sitting room, where we have a few sing-alongs and generally chill out," Liz said. "We try to make music and art a part of everyday life here. The children seem to love it, and some of the work they produce is incredible."

"Yes, so I see," Mrs. Grace said, looking at the framed pictures hanging along the walls. "These are beautiful. Look at the color and movement!"

"I love this one!" Josie exclaimed, pointing at a wonderfully detailed and intricate pen-and-ink sketch of the front of Friendship House. "It must have had been done by a professional artist, though."

"You'd think so, wouldn't you?" said Liz, looking over her shoulder. "In fact, that picture was drawn by a fourteen-year-old boy. He can't read or write, but he's fascinated by buildings, and he can draw them like you wouldn't believe."

"It's incredible!" Josie cried, examining the picture even more closely and then turning to look at Liz in surprise.

"Great, isn't it?" Liz said proudly. "I tell you, I'm always finding myself amazed here. Billy's an exception, of course, but all of the children seem to enjoy their sessions so much. I'd really like to get an art teacher to help us, though that's just one of my dreams at the moment. Now," she went on, "let me show you the studio where it all happens. Then we can see the children's rooms and I'll take you outside for a look at the field and the stables."

They followed Liz around the building, while she told them about the children who came to stay there and the kinds of things they enjoyed doing. The more she talked, the more enthusiastic she became, and Josie realized that working at Friendship House was more than just a job for Liz—it was her whole life.

"You've got fantastic facilities here," Mrs. Grace said, as they walked through one of the bedrooms in the modern extension. Most of the rooms had two or three beds, but some were just for one person, and there was an assistant's room at the end of each corridor.

"I know, we're lucky, aren't we?" Liz replied. "The center was set up by a wealthy couple with a physically challenged daughter who discovered what a huge need there was for a place like this, and we've kept going by private donations ever since. Most of the families whose children come here give us something, but we don't insist if they can't afford it. Now, follow me, and I'll show you one of my favorite places."

She opened a door at the back of the building and led Josie and her mother through to a wide terrace. There were more pots spilling over with flowers all the way along it, and beyond lay a small field in which two donkeys were grazing.

"Jack and Jill," Liz said, waving an arm toward them. "Not very original, I'm afraid! Over there"— she pointed across the paddock to a large wire enclosure with several hutches in it—"we've got the rabbits and guinea pigs. The stables are on the other side, at the back of the main house. It used to be a coaching inn, and three of the old stalls are left. Shall we go and say hello to the donkeys first?"

"Yes, please," Josie said eagerly.

"I always like bringing the children out here," Liz said, following on behind her with Mrs. Grace. "Meeting the animals really seems to help if they feel homesick or lonely—and many of them do, at first."

"Oh, I love donkeys," Josie said, as she reached the fence and the two of them trotted toward her. "It's just something about their furry ears. . . ."

"I know exactly what you mean," Mrs. Grace said, feeling in her jacket pocket for a sugar lump. "Who looks after them?" she asked, turning to Liz. "You probably don't have enough time!"

"No, I don't," Liz answered. "We've got a couple of men in charge of the grounds and the building, and Sid, the older one, takes care of the two of them. They're his pride and joy! I'm sorry he's not here at the moment, or he'd talk to you about them for hours. He's been nagging me for months about getting a horse for the children to ride."

Josie and her mother both looked at Liz, aware that they were getting to the heart of the matter. "So, tell us more about what you're looking for," Mrs. Grace asked her.

"Well, anyone who works here needs to be very

even tempered," Liz replied, scratching a donkey's nose. "Some of the children can be quite noisy, particularly when they're excited, and we couldn't risk having an animal who might hurt them out of fear. And to be honest, trotting around and giving rides isn't the most exciting thing in the world, so a high-spirited horse would probably go crazy with boredom. But some horses seem to thrive on it. Somehow they realize they have to be patient, and they'll put up with almost anything."

She smiled sympathetically, looking at Josie's thoughtful face. "There's a lot for you to think over," she said. "I realize you might have been imagining your horse would go to a family, rather than somewhere like here. Why don't I leave you both to have a chat? You can wander around and explore. Come and find me inside when you're ready." And without further delay, she strode back off toward the modern building.

"Well, where do you want to go first?" Mrs. Grace asked Josie as they watched Liz's determined back disappear into the distance. "Rabbits or stables?"

"Stables," Josie said promptly. "That's really what we're here for, after all."

They walked back along the terrace, looking out at the peaceful scene. Behind the rabbits' enclosure was a swing set that faced toward the field. Jack and Jill were now standing under a large oak tree in one corner, their gray coats perfectly camouflaged against its trunk.

"I wonder how many horses have been put up here over the years?" Mrs. Grace said as they approached the row of stalls that were covered by a mossy tiled roof. She peered into the dark stables. "Just imagine what it must have been like—passengers sleeping in the inn while the horses stayed out here, then harnessed up and off again in the morning. More exciting than catching the train! A lot slower, too, though."

"Come on, Mom," Josie said, tapping her back. "Stop trying to avoid the issue. What do you think of Friendship House?"

"I think it's a wonderful place," Mrs. Grace replied, turning around to lean against the stable door and look along the terrace. "Liz is great, and the grounds are perfect."

"But . . ." Josie prompted. "There is a 'but' in your voice—I can hear it."

"Okay," her mother smiled. "I've got two 'buts,' I suppose. First, we really can't tell how Hope is going to react to the children. We're assuming she'll be fine, because she's so calm, but we don't know for certain. She hasn't really had any experience with handicapped people—Grace's Stables have always been too small for that."

"Oh, Mom, I'm sure she'll be perfectly happy," Josie protested. "Remember me telling you how calm she was when those boys were bothering me and Anna? I bet none of the children can yell any louder than that bike horn!"

"Yes, but you know horses. They're just like people, with their own funny little likes and dislikes," Mrs. Grace replied. "It may be that Hope won't respond as well as we expect, that's all I'm saying." She put her arm around Josie's shoulder, and they began to walk back toward the house.

"Well, I still think you're worrying about nothing," Josie replied. "Anyway, what's the second problem?"

"Well, what if Liz decides she doesn't want Hope once she sees her, like the Simmondses did?" Mrs.

Grace said, frowning into the distance. "I can't bear it when people reject her. I think I'd rather let her go to the sanctuary now than risk that again. At least Mrs. Peabody loves animals for what they are."

"Oh, but so would Liz!" Josie exclaimed. "I'm certain of it. She's wouldn't judge on appearances. You can tell that just by talking to her for five minutes."

"Yes, you're probably right," her mother said, thinking it over. "But with the sweet itch, too—" Then, she suddenly clapped one hand to her forehead and said, "Of course—I keep forgetting to tell you, Josie! The spray you found on the Internet arrived yesterday! With Mrs. Peabody being there when you got back from school, it went right out of my head, and then you rushed off before I could talk to you this morning."

"So what's it like?" Josie asked eagerly. "Have you been using it?"

"Well, it's too early to tell for sure, but I've been spraying Hope every few hours and I think it might—just might—be making a difference," Mrs. Grace said. "Her skin certainly isn't getting any worse."

"Yes!" Josie said, feeling a tingle of excitement. "Everything's going to work out, I know it will!"

"Now look, sweetie," Mrs. Grace said seriously, "I don't want you to get too carried away, in case we're disappointed again. Maybe Friendship House *is* the right place for Hope, but there's still an awful lot to be decided."

"Then let's go and find Liz and start talking!" Josie said, propelling her mother with a firm hand on her shoulder toward the back door of the main building.

"Don't you want to see the rabbits and guinea pigs?" Mrs. Grace asked, laughing, as she was pushed along.

"No, I don't!" Josie replied firmly. "How can we possibly think about rabbits and guinea pigs at a time like this? Hope's future is lying in the balance!"

They found Liz in the kitchen, sitting on a stool and talking to an older woman in overalls. "This is Joan," she said. "She handles all our catering—and she does a fantastic job, too." Everyone smiled and said hello, then Joan made a pot of tea before disappearing off to the dining room.

"So," Liz said, "what do you two think? Would Hope be happy here? Tell me more about her."

"We *think* that she would," Mrs. Grace said cautiously, taking a sip from her cup. "She's a very gentle, calm creature, and nothing usually bothers her. But as I was saying to Josie, she hasn't come across physically challenged children before, so we can't be absolutely sure how she'll react."

"We're ninety-nine percent sure, though!" Josie put in, worried that her mother sounded too pessimistic. "At least, I am. Hope's the most wonderful horse, Liz—she's so kind and patient, and she's marvelous with beginners."

"Well, she sounds perfect!" Liz smiled.

"Josie!" said her mother, shooting her a warning look. "What did I say about getting your hopes up?" She turned to Liz. "*We* think Hope's lovely because we know her so well, but I ought to tell you that you could probably find a prettier horse. Hope's a sweetheart, but she's no great beauty. And at the moment, she's having a few problems with a skin complaint—"

"Though that's improving," Josie added hurriedly.

"Plus, she's a bit stocky with quite a broad back," Mrs. Grace went on, determined that everything should be out in the open.

"Then she really *is* perfect!" Liz said, laughing. "That's just what most of our children need. A lot of them have problems with their vision, and what they want is a solid base to sit on. Helps with their balance. And for goodness' sake—as if I cared about her looks! I can tell you that none of the kids will, for a single second."

"Well, then," Mrs. Grace said thankfully, "perhaps you could bring some of them around to meet her."

"I'd love to," Liz said, jumping off her stool. "I'll go and get my calendar from the office and we can fix it up. Oh, I've got a good feeling in my bones about this!"

"Yes," said Josie, beaming at her. "So do I!"

CHAPTER EIGHT

"Let's get this muck out of here," said Ben, wheeling the barrow and its towering load of dirty straw away from the stalls.

"Thanks, Ben," Josie said, coming out of Charity's stall and rubbing her aching shoulders. She leaned against the wall and took a few minutes out to watch everyone else working.

It was Sunday afternoon, and lessons had finished half an hour earlier. Grace's Stables was a hive of activity: Ben and Anna were busy mucking out the stables and grooming the horses. Lynne Marshall had come over to help Robert Grace paint the scenery for the musical—after he'd spent fifteen minutes charming her into it over the phone. She and Josie's mom were now unloading overalls, brushes, tins, and cans of spray paint from her van and taking them to the barn, where the painting would take place.

"That's it, I think," Lynne called, on her way up there with a final load of buckets, rags, and sponges. "We should have everything we need."

"Then I'd say it was time for a break," Mary Grace replied, appearing from the barn. "Come on, you need to keep your strength up, and I feel like a chat. It seems like months since I've seen you."

"Break?" Robert Grace said indignantly as they added more equipment to the pile on the barn floor. "But we're just ready to start! You're not due a break for at least another couple of hours."

"Slave driver!" Lynne called back, as she and Mary began to walk over to School Farm. "We won't be long, I promise!"

Josie smiled and went to see if she could help Anna groom Hope.

"Don't you think the two of us are incredibly brilliant?" Anna asked as she came over.

"Well, we are, of course," Josie replied, "but for any reason in particular?"

"Check out Hope's mane," Anna replied, pointing toward it with a body brush. "Is that spray making a difference, or what?" The spots had nearly disappeared, and the dark, shabby patches on Hope's light coat were fading as new hair grew over them.

"I know, it's great," Josie said with satisfaction, as she stroked Hope's neck. "I thought her coat was improving yesterday, and today it's even better. Mom's taking photos every day to send back to the person who's developed the formula, and she's keeping a diary, too."

"It would be good to get the sweet itch solved before Hope's sold," Anna said. "Do you think she's really got a chance of going to Friendship House?" Josie had told her all about the place.

"We'll have to see how she gets along with the children," Josie said, looking anxiously over at the yard. "They should be coming any minute."

"Oh, I'm going to miss her so much," Anna said, throwing her arms around Hope's neck and giving her a big hug.

"We all will," Josie said sadly. "Still, she's got to go somewhere, and Friendship House is near enough for visits."

"Sorry, Josie," Anna said, looking around at her. "Here I go again—making you feel worse. Mom keeps telling me to think about other people's feelings, but I just can't seem to help blurting things out." She put her arm around Josie's shoulders. "So, tell me, how are *you* finding all this?" she asked solemnly. "Is there anything you'd like to share with me?"

"Oh, stop!" Josie said, laughing and shrugging her arm away. "I think I like the old, tactless Anna better!"

She took another body brush from the kit in Charity's stall and began to untangle Hope's tail a section at a time. "But, since you asked," she went on, "I'm not really sure how I feel. Half the time I worry that friendship house might be the perfect place for Hope but that for some reason she won't be able to go there. And then, the rest of the time I think that they'll want to have her but she won't be happy, surrounded by lots of noisy children."

"Well, it's nearly make-your-mind-up time," Anna said. "Look, here they come."

They watched as a white minivan with FRIENDSHIP HOUSE painted on the side pulled up and parked in the yard.

"Why don't you go out and meet them?" Anna said to Josie. "I'll get your mom from the house." And she set off toward the path to School Farm.

Liz Tallant was climbing out of the driver's seat of the minivan, and she smiled and waved when she saw Josie coming over. A couple of other adults were already starting to open the doors and help the children out, and soon a small group was standing in the yard.

"I won't introduce you to everyone right away— you're bound to forget all the names," Liz said to Josie. "But these are the lucky few who most wanted to meet Hope, and Marion and Pete who've come to help."

"Hello, there," Josie said brightly, to a little girl of seven or eight who was holding Liz's hand tightly. At once, she shrank back and hid her face.

"Sarah's feeling a bit shy at the moment," Liz explained. "She's going to stick very close to me."

Just then Mrs. Grace and Anna appeared, and Ben came over, and soon the ice was broken and everyone was chatting. The children were beginning to wander off in different directions, so Josie's mom made a suggestion, "Why don't we go and say hello to Hope now? She's over here, ready and waiting."

Josie smiled at the tall girl standing next to her, not quite sure whether she should offer to help. "It's this way," she said. "Shall we go together?"

"Yes!" said the girl firmly, taking hold of Josie's hand in her own much larger one. "My name's Cathy. What's yours? I've brought my bag with all my special things. Do you want to know what they are?"

"Yes, please," Josie said, delighted that Cathy was so easy to talk to. They obviously weren't going to have a problem making conversation.

"Tommy! What are you up to?" Liz suddenly called to a dark-haired boy who had started to chase after a couple of hens. They squawked in alarm and scattered across the yard, much to his obvious delight.

"Don't frighten those poor chickens!" Liz said to him, but Anna was already on her way over. "I think you'd better come with me, Tommy," she said, taking his arm. "I've got a brother, and I know just what to do with rowdy boys."

"Rowdy boys!" Tommy crowed, grinning wildly and clapping. Anna laughed and towed him off, while Ben followed on behind, promising to get even.

"Why don't you tell us about Hope, Josie?" Liz suggested, walking along beside her with Sarah.

"Well, my mom bought her at an auction nine years ago, when I was three," Josie began, aware of Cathy and Sarah listening intently. "We already had a horse called Faith, who isn't here anymore—"

"Is she dead?" Cathy asked seriously.

"No, she's just gone to a new home," Josie reassured her. "Anyway, Mom thought Faith was bound to get along with a horse called Hope, because they had the same sort of name. And she liked her anyway, because she looked so calm and gentle."

Cathy smiled approvingly. "That's nice," she said, shifting her bag to the other shoulder.

"Then Hope began to get fatter and fatter," Josie went on. "Nobody could figure out why, until the vet told us she was going to have a foal. And a few months later she gave birth to Charity." By now they'd reached the stalls, and she added, "Charity's in the stable and this is Hope, tied up outside. Would you like to pat her?"

"No, I'll just look for now," Cathy said, quite contentedly. "I've got some special things in my bag and I don't want them to get broken."

So Josie hung back with Cathy and watched as the children surrounded Hope—all patting, stroking, talking, and laughing, at once. Josie held her breath. How would the horse react? There was such a lot of noise and movement! But Hope patiently stood still, only sometimes lifting her head away from the more eager arms that were stretching up to her.

And then, overcome with excitement, Tommy let out a high squeal—so loud that it made Josie jump. The other children were startled into silence. Charity, who had been watching everything that was going on over her stable door, snorted in alarm and retreated to the depths of her stall. Hope, though, just took one step backward and shook her head a couple of times as she avoided Tommy's waving hand.

"Do you like dogs, too?" Anna asked, taking him quietly away. "There's a nice dog called Basil somewhere around. Shall we go and find him?"

"Well!" Liz said to Josie. "Hope really is a

superstar! You weren't exaggerating when you said how special she was."

Josie just smiled. There was something about seeing Hope standing there with the children that filled her with a pride she couldn't quite express.

"Would you like to pat the horse now, Sarah?" Liz said, bending down. "Come on, she's lovely!" Gently, she led her forward into a space among the other children. Then, taking her hand, she guided it toward Hope's neck, and Josie realized with a shock that Sarah was blind.

She watched as the little girl began to stroke Hope—timidly at first, then gradually becoming more confident. Her tight, anxious face began to relax as she concentrated on the feeling of the horse's silky, warm skin under her fingers. Fascinated, she began to explore Hope's mane, and Josie could imagine just what a surprise the thicker, wiry hair there must be to Sarah.

Hope turned her head around and gently blew down her nose, sniffing at Sarah's hand. Josie felt Liz take an anxious breath, and Sarah froze for a second that seemed to last for minutes. Then her intent face broke into a beaming smile. "It tickles!" she said.

"Does it?" Liz said delightedly. "Do you like it?"

"Yes!" Sarah said, and laughed.

Liz turned to Josie and whispered, "That's the first thing she's said since she arrived yesterday morning."

Josie had to bite her lip to stop that choking feeling in her throat. She was glad to hurry away to grab a couple of hard hats from the tack room when her mother suggested the children might like to take turns having horse rides.

From that moment on, the visit turned into a huge success. All the children who wanted to had a ride on Hope, and she carried them as steadily and patiently as Josie had thought she would. Those who weren't riding explored the stables. They were fascinated by the tack room, and loved watching the ducks on the pond. The Graces' cats, Millie and Rascal, kept well out of the way, but Basil was another big hit—particularly with Tommy. He and Anna spent ages throwing a tennis ball for the terrier to fetch, though it was difficult for Tommy to control his arm movements and it was anybody's guess where the ball would end up. Both he and

Anna thought this was a great joke, and they were soon laughing hysterically together.

Later, while they were all standing together having a drink in the sunshine, Liz suddenly looked around the group and said, "Hang on, we're missing a couple of people. Where are Cathy and Mark?" Then her anxious expression relaxed a little as she added, "Oh, Marion's not here, either—she's probably with them. Still, I think I'd better go and see what they're up to."

"I'll come with you," Josie offered, "just in case you get lost."

They looked in the outdoor schooling ring, the tack room, and the office, and down at the duck pond, without any success.

"I know!" Josie said, as a thought occurred to her. "Let's try the barn. My dad and our friend Lynne are painting in there. Perhaps the others are with them."

They hurried past the stalls toward the big covered building and, sure enough, the sound of several voices came from inside. Propped against a couple of hay bales at the barn entrance was the plywood cutout of a long, flashy car. It was shiny with silver foil metalwork and metallic red paint, and the words "Greased Lightning" ran along the side. Robert Grace and one of the boys from Friendship House were crouched at one end, carefully spray-painting the front wheel.

"Lee! That's fantastic!" Liz exclaimed, but he was too absorbed even to turn around.

"Lee's been a great help," Mr. Grace beamed, putting down the can and coming over. "We needed someone who knew a bit about cars and, as if by magic, there he was!"

"This is my dad, Robert Grace," Josie said, introducing him to Liz. "He's putting on a musical next week—no prizes for guessing which one."

"We've roped in Cathy, too," Mr. Grace said cheerfully, shaking hands and then waving an arm behind him into the barn. "She and Lynne are in charge of the backdrop for our American diner."

"Lynne is Anna and Ben's mother," Josie explained, as Liz looked across to see her and Cathy busy painting a huge sheet of canvas that was draped over some more hay bales. Lynne stopped to explain something to Cathy, waving big circles on the air with her brush. "She's an artist," Josie added, in case Liz thought she was just rather eccentric.

"She's been marvelous," put in Marion, the helper, coming over. "Both the children are in seventh heaven. You know what Lee's like about cars, and Cathy's even given me her bag so she has both hands free. Sorry, I should have come over and told you where we were."

"Oh, don't worry about that," Liz said, still watching Lynne intently. "It's great to see them so happy." Then she turned back to Josie and said, "I'm glad you brought me here. I've got a feeling Lynne and I should have a chat before we leave. It could turn out to be quite interesting for both of us!"

CHAPTER NINE

"I feel worn out!" Josie groaned, resting her head in her arms on the kitchen table.

"That makes two of us," said her mother, yawning. "But we have been on the go since early this morning, after all."

"Is anyone else a little bit hungry?" Ben asked hopefully, looking around the empty kitchen for any sign of food.

"Ben!" Anna and her mother exclaimed together, while Mr. Grace smiled and went to get the Chinese takeout menu down from the bulletin board. "Let's have your orders!" he said, looking at the exhausted group around the kitchen table.

"Beef and broccoli, please," Ben replied

promptly, "and spring rolls to start off with."

"The usual, please, Dad—sweet and sour pork," Josie asked, while Anna requested shrimp dumplings, chicken with cashew nuts, and a noodle dish for Lynne, who was vegetarian.

"And for you, madam?" Robert Grace asked his wife, with a pencil poised over a piece of scrap paper.

"Oh, I'll have anything, thanks," Mrs. Grace replied, wrinkling her nose. "I'm a bit sick of takeout, to be honest. The sooner this musical of yours is finished, Rob, the better, as far as I'm concerned."

"Well, you only have to wait until Friday," Mr. Grace said, studying the menu. "I'll get going on Saturday with the party food, and it'll be good home cooking from then on, I promise. Oh, before I forget—I invited Liz to the party."

"Great," Josie said. "I think she's really nice."

"Yes, and she's going to bring the children, too," her father added as an afterthought, scribbling down his order.

"Rob!" Mrs. Grace said, staring at him in alarm. "How many children is she bringing? Will we have enough food? Not to mention enough room?"

"Oh, relax," he said airily, "it'll be fine. You worry too much. The best parties are always crowded, and you can leave the food to me." Then suddenly he stopped writing down numbers from the menu and looked up, a gleam in his eye. "Of course!" he said. "I'll get the cast to come in costume, and they can perform a couple of songs. The kids will love it!"

Mrs. Grace just shook her head, lost for words. Lynne laughed and lay a hand over her friend's. "Give in gracefully and let him do it," she advised.

"People are going to talk about this party for years to come," Mr. Grace said happily. "A live performance will be the finishing touch!"

"So, how is the musical going?" Lynne asked, dabbing halfheartedly at the spot of paint she'd just noticed on her denim shirt.

"Well, I *think* it's finally all coming together," he replied. "There are a couple more songs we need to work on, but the dancing is fantastic now. They're really catchy tunes, and Jane and I have worked out some great moves. She's the music teacher, by the way. You should see the roller-skating waitresses in the diner!"

"We will see them," Josie reminded him. "We're coming to the opening night, remember? On Wednesday?"

"Sounds cool," Anna said. "Can we come too?"

"Of course," said Mr. Grace, going out to the hall to phone the restaurant. "Your mother's the official set designer. Tickets are on the house."

"Come on, Mom," Josie said, while they waited for her father to return with the food. "You still haven't told us how you left things with Liz. What did she say? Does she want Hope?"

"Yes, she does," Mrs. Grace replied. "She thought Hope was wonderful, and she'd really like to buy her. But she wants us to be absolutely sure in our own minds that it's the right thing to do. So, what does everyone think?"

"Well, *I'd* say—" Anna began, before catching sight of her mother's face and biting back the words. "How do you feel about it, Josie?" she asked instead, and Lynne smiled her approval.

"I'm *almost* sure that Hope ought to go to Friendship House," Josie said carefully. "It was really moving seeing her with the children, wasn't it?

Nothing seemed to bother her."

"I know what you mean," Ben said. "I was watching her, and she was even more gentle with them than she is with beginners at the stables here. It's like she has some sixth sense that tells her they need some help."

"Even that little blind girl plucked up the courage to go for a ride," Mrs. Grace added. "She just loved Hope, didn't she? The look on her face when she was sitting up in the saddle so proudly nearly broke my heart!"

"Don't, Mom," Josie said. "You'll set me off again." She jumped up to start setting the table. Then she went on, "I would like to know more about how they'd look after her, though. Who's going to groom and feed her? Her sweet itch does seem to be almost better, thankfully, but it still needs a careful eye kept on it. And would there be anybody to take her out for a good long ride every now and then? I'm sure she'll need it."

"I talked to Liz about all of that while we were having tea," Mrs. Grace replied. "She does know something about horses herself, through work she's done with horses and physically challenged children, but Sid would be mainly looking after them. He's the groundskeeper in charge of the donkeys," she explained for Ben and Anna's benefit, "and a real animal lover, apparently. He's been suggesting they get a horse for ages."

"Do you think Liz would let us come and take Hope out sometimes?" Anna asked, reaching into the cupboard for glasses while Ben looked for cans of cold drinks in the fridge. By now, they were as familiar with the kitchen at School Farm as their own.

"I'm sure she wouldn't mind if you came to ride her," Mrs. Grace said, "though it might be difficult for you to get up there regularly. Friendship House is about half an hour away by car."

"What sort of place is it?" Lynne asked casually. "Liz seems so nice, I'd imagine the children love being there."

"When we saw it, none of them were around," Mary Grace replied. "Even so, you can tell the place has a really good atmosphere. There's a happy feel to it—the rooms are all bright and cheerful."

"The children have done some of the most amazing paintings," Josie put in, setting down the last fork. "And the studio is terrific! There's even a kiln for firing pots. You ought to go and have a look some time, Lynne."

"Yes, maybe I will," she murmured.

Anna looked at her curiously as she searched in the cupboard for some soy sauce. "Are you planning something, Mom?" she asked.

"Oh, not really," Lynne answered vaguely. "Anyway, let's get back to the point. It certainly sounds as though Hope would be well looked after. But do you think she'd be happy?"

"I bet she would," Anna said. "She'd have the donkeys to keep her company, and lots of attention. I say we should let her go to Friendship House—I think they deserve her. A lot more than Emma Price, anyway."

"I'll second that," said Ben, while his mother added, "And I vote in favor."

Mrs. Grace looked at Josie. "Do you agree?" she asked her. "We need you on our side, too."

"I think it's the best option," Josie replied, thinking everything over for the hundredth time. "After all, aside from the sanctuary, this is her last hope, isn't it?"

"That's settled, then," her mother said. "Don't worry, Josie, I'm sure Hope will love it at Friendship House. As soon as I saw her with Liz and all the others this afternoon, I felt it was the perfect place for her."

"Yes, you're probably right," Josie said, trying her best to feel cheerful and almost succeeding.

The next few days seemed to pass in a blur, which was almost a relief for Josie. Now that they'd decided on Hope's new home, she was anxious to get her settled in at Friendship House. If there were going to be any problems, it would be better to know about them sooner rather than later.

Mrs. Grace had called Liz Tallant on Monday to say they'd be delighted to accept her offer, and it was arranged that she and Josie would bring Hope around on Sunday, the day after the party. "That's if we all survive it," she said darkly to Josie. "As far as I can make out, your father's invited anyone who's ever set foot in the stables, plus most of his school. I don't know where we're going to put them all. If it's raining, we're finished!"

Then, before Josie knew it, Wednesday had arrived and they were setting off with Lynne and the twins for the opening night of *Grease*.

"I don't know about Rob, but I'm certainly feeling nervous," Mrs. Grace said as they sat on rows of chairs in the packed school hall. "I hope the musical's a smash—he's put so much effort into it."

"I'm sure it's going to be great, Mom," Josie reassured her. "Dad's productions always are."

"And even if it's not, in a couple of days it'll all be over," said Anna, from the next seat. "Just think—you won't have to listen to 'Summer Lovin' ' ever again."

"Shh!" Josie whispered, giggling, as the lights dimmed and a band began to play. "It's about to begin!"

The black curtains in front of the stage began to open, and there was a gasp from the audience as the opening scene was revealed. About twenty students were arranged in two groups on the steps leading up to the high-school entrance. The girls were all wearing tight-fitting tops and brightly colored, bouncy skirts that swirled out from wide belts at the waist. They sat to one side, while the boys in leather jackets, sunglasses, and greased-back hair swaggered around on the other.

"Wow!" Lynne breathed admiringly. "Great costumes!"

"Great set design," Josie said, smiling at her.

"Great music!" Anna added, as the strains of "Summer Lovin'" filled the hall, and Josie snorted with laughter so loudly that her mother had to glare.

"I think you could say the musical's more than just a success," Lynne said to Mary Grace as they all lined up for drinks during the intermission. "It's a complete and utter triumph!"

"I know," she agreed happily. "Thank goodness for that! The dancing is amazing, and we've still got the roller-skating waitresses to come."

"Oh, yeah, in the diner," Josie said. "I want to see the backdrop you were painting with Cathy, Lynne."

"As a matter of fact, I've got something to tell you all which is connected with that," Lynne said mysteriously. "I didn't want to say anything until it was settled."

"I knew it!" Anna pounced on her mother. "I could tell you were hatching some little scheme.

Come on, Mom—out with it! What have you been up to?"

"Well, I've got a new job," said Lynne, looking very pleased with herself. "At Friendship House. I'm going to run the art sessions there."

"Congratulations!" Mary Grace said. "What wonderful news! When did you fix all that up?"

"I talked to Liz on Sunday when we were in the barn," Lynne told her, "and she invited me over on Monday to see the studio and to have an interview. This morning she called to say the trustees have agreed to appoint me. I can't wait to start. I did an art therapy course at college, you see."

"That's great," Josie said, delighted. "I can just see you at Friendship House—it's exactly your kind of place."

"Congratulations!" said Ben, and Anna gave their mom a hug. "It sounds perfect," she said. "You won't be so tired, and maybe you'll have a bit more time to paint, too." Then suddenly she grabbed Josie's arm in excitement.

"That's it!" she exclaimed, so loudly that several people turned around to look. "Of course! This means we'll be able to keep in touch with Hope!

We'll know if she's happy or not, and over the holidays, we can go with Mom and exercise her. I'm sure Liz won't mind. Oh, what could be better?"

"I couldn't possibly imagine!" said Josie, with a broad grin.

CHAPTER
TEN

Josie sat on the desk in her bedroom, her back against the corner wall and her feet on a chair, and looked out of the window. Hope and Charity were standing in the field below. Lessons for the weekend had finished that Saturday morning, and now the stables were closed to give everyone time to prepare for the party. Josie smiled as she saw Hope move closer to Charity and begin to groom her, as she scratched and nibbled her withers. Charity stood still at first, then eventually walked away, tired of being fussed over. Never mind, Hope, Josie said to herself, just wait until you see those two donkeys in your new field. They're going to need a lot of looking after. The motherly horse swished her tail a couple of times, gazing after Charity, then dropped her head and began grazing again.

Josie sighed, looking around her room for something to do. Ben and Anna and their mother were coming over later to help decorate the stables, and she didn't feel like starting the job without them. Her father had gone out shopping early that morning and had come back with the car piled high with bulging grocery bags. They'd had a quick sandwich for lunch, and then he'd shooed Josie and her mother out of the way. Enticing smells had already begun to waft up the stairs.

Josie decided to go down and see if he needed a hand. "How's it going, Dad?" she asked, wandering into the kitchen. "Do you want some help?"

Her father turned around from the stove, his face red and a stripe of flour on his cheek. "Oh, hi, sweetheart," he said distractedly. "Let me think— what's left to do? Chicken's in the oven, the pies are next, hot dogs and pizza we won't cook until later. How about cookies? Or, you can make angel food cake. Yes, that's a good idea. Eggs in the fridge— we'll need about two dozen to start off with, if they'll fit in the bowl." He rushed over to the cupboard and reached down a couple of bowls and cups. "They'll need separating," he instructed Josie. "Whites in the big bowl, yolks in the smaller one. Better break the whites into this bowl first, in case some of the yolk gets in by mistake."

"Okay," Josie said, taking two large egg cartons out of the fridge. She began to crack the first smooth shell on the side of one of the bowls, and dig in her thumbs to break the two halves apart. "I thought *Grease* was great, Dad," she said, slopping the yolk from one eggshell cup to the other. "I haven't really seen you since, to tell you. Is the entire cast coming to the party?"

"Most of them," said her father distractedly, flipping over pages in a recipe book.

"The girl who was playing Sandy has a great voice," Josie went on. "She's not so good at dancing, though, is she?"

"Mmm," her father replied, reaching past her to the cupboard above the work surface.

"Uh-oh," Josie said, fishing into the big bowl. "I've got a little bit of yolk in this egg white. Now how did that happen? D'you think it'll matter? It's only a little bit . . ."

"Josie," her father said firmly, taking the bowl out of her hands, "thanks for the offer, dear, but I think I'm better off on my own. I've got to concentrate, or I'll never get anything done. Why don't you see where Mom is?"

"Oh, okay," Josie said. "If you're sure." But he was already busy fishing yolk out of the bowl and didn't reply.

She ambled out to the yard and caught sight of her mother's bent head through the tack room window.

"What are you doing cleaning tack, Mom?" she asked, putting her head around the door. "Why don't you leave that until tomorrow?"

"Well, we're taking Hope to Friendship House in the morning," her mother replied. "Might as well give this bridle a good polish now. Don't want her to start off on the wrong foot!" And she smiled rather sadly.

Josie sighed again and slumped on to a stool. "This is so weird," she said. "Everyone's busy but I can't think of anything to do except sit here and wait. Wait for everyone to arrive and the party to start. Wait for Hope to go off to her new home. In some ways, I wish it was all over."

Her mother looked at her sympathetically. "You're bound to be feeling a bit strange," she said. "I do, too. After all, everything's beginning to wind down, with Connie and Tubber having gone to Littlehaven yesterday and Hope going away tomorrow. That leaves us with just Charity. This party is a kind of a good-bye to the stables, isn't it?"

"Are you still going to give lessons with Charity?" Josie asked. She hadn't really considered what would happen after Hope left the riding school.

"Well, maybe for a few more weeks," her mother replied, rubbing the bit vigorously with some metal polish. "Felicity wants to continue on for as long as possible, and some of the other students might, too. The thing is, Dad and I really ought to start house hunting, now the show's done with. It's not that long until we have to be out of here."

"Oh," said Josie, thinking it over. It still seemed amazing that they were going to be moving out of School Farm. She'd lived there all her life.

"Don't forget what Dad said in the office," Mrs. Grace reminded Josie, giving her hand a squeeze.

"We've got each other, and that's the main thing. Everything else is going to work out okay."

"And you've got us, too!" came a cheerful voice through the door. It was Anna, her arms full of bunting and packets of balloons and streamers. She tried out a blower that unrolled to reveal a bright red feather at the end. "Come on, Josie—there's work to do!"

"Well, I think you've done a great job with the yard," said Mr. Grace, looking around a couple of hours later. "It looks great!"

Brightly colored bunting zigzagged across from the stalls over to the office and tack room on the other side, and balloons were pinned up everywhere. Mrs. Grace was always worried about fire risks, so outdoor candles and lanterns were stuck safely in buckets of sand, ready to be lit later on. The "Greased Lightning" car was back at the barn, propped up by the entrance next to a huge stereo sound system that Mr. Grace had borrowed from the music department. Lynne Marshall had also brought along several picnic tables in her van. Now they stood in a line along one side of the yard, covered by bottles, paper plates, and cups, alongside huge bowls and platters of food shrouded under plastic wrap.

"You've outdone yourself, Rob," said Mrs. Grace admiringly. "I've never seen so much delicious-looking food!"

"There's plenty more in the kitchen," he said. "We'll just have to go back for more supplies when they're needed." He turned to Josie, Ben, and Anna. "Could you three keep an eye on people's glasses and go around with bottles if they need a refill?"

"Sure, Dad," Josie replied, when an idea struck her. "I know! Why don't your roller-skating waitresses help as well?"

"I'm not so sure about that," her father replied with a smile. "Judging from the number of near misses we had on stage, I think it might be better if they just stood in a corner somewhere until it's time for their number. I'd rather rely on you, if you don't mind."

"Maybe we should try a few dishes first," Ben suggested, lifting up the corner of a cover and stealing a hot dog. "So we'll know what to recommend."

"Ben! Don't eat everything before people start arriving," Lynne scolded.

"Oh, help yourself," Mr. Grace replied in his usual laid-back way. "We may be too busy soon." He reached under the table and brought out a couple of bottles. "And now we're all together and it's just family, so to speak, I think it's time for a toast."

He lined up some glasses. The six of them held up their glasses and clinked them together as he announced, "To the future, whatever it holds!"

"And let's toast to Hope," Josie added. "This is her last night here, remember."

They looked over to the stalls and burst out laughing. "Oh, Anna!" Mrs. Grace said. "What have you been up to?"

Apples, carrots, and turnips had been hung across the lower part of the stable doors, and Hope and Charity were busy nibbling them off their strings.

"Well, we're having fun—why shouldn't they?" Anna protested. "It's their party, too!"

"And here come the first arrivals," said Mr. Grace, going forward to meet a group of people who were walking up the drive. "Now let's just enjoy ourselves and forget everything for a few hours."

"Sounds good to me," Josie said, feeling her spirits beginning to lift. "I think we deserve some fun!"

"Josie, can you give me a hand, please?" Mr. Grace said, rushing over to where she was standing, chatting to Jill Atterbury. "Sorry to interrupt, but we need more soft drinks from the kitchen."

"Sure," Josie said. "Don't go away, Jill, I'll see you in a minute." She hurried up the path to the house with her father.

"Seems to be going well, doesn't it?" he said. "The joint's jumping."

"Oh, Dad, it's great," Josie said. "There are so many people here! I never knew Jill was going to come. And guess what? She was telling me she might be able to start riding Faith sidesaddle before too much longer. It won't put so much strain on her hip, apparently. Isn't that fantastic?"

"It's a great idea," Mr. Grace said as they came into the kitchen. He started piling bottles into Josie's outstretched arms. "Nearly all the cast has turned up, too," he added. "And the Friendship House children should be here soon. I've told Liz she can bring the minivan right into the yard. Then we can get the singing and dancing going."

"I bet they'll love that," Josie said.

"Seeing Hope again is going to be a treat for them, too. After all, they've gotten to know her a little bit now," her father added, as he found a case of sodas from under the table and led the way out of the kitchen.

"I suppose so," Josie said, a little more doubtfully than she'd intended.

"What's the matter, sweet pea?" her father asked, pausing to turn and look back at her. "You *are* feeling okay about Hope going there, aren't you? You were so excited about Friendship House at first, but you don't seem so certain now."

"Oh, I don't know—it's hard to explain," Josie said with a sigh as they walked on down the path to the yard. "I can see Hope giving the children rides and everything, and I'm sure she'll be very good with them. She likes working and being useful. It's just that she's been our pet, too, hasn't she? One of the family. I'm sure she'll be a part of the team at Friendship House, but do you think they'll really love her?"

"Something tells me you don't need to worry about that," said Mr. Grace slowly. He nodded his head toward the yard. "Take a look over there, and I think you'll find the answer to your question."

The Friendship House minivan was parked in the far corner, and Josie saw her mother standing next to it, talking to Liz Tallant. Over at the stalls, Hope was surrounded by several excited children. Tommy was standing stock-still, his face buried in her mane and his arms around her neck. A girl was stroking her soft muzzle and Cathy was patting her plain workhorse nose and kissing it over and over again. Hope's eyes were closed and she looked blissfully happy.

Anna came up from the crowded yard and stood next to Josie, watching the scene with her. "I'd say that was a horse in seventh heaven!" Anna said. "She's the center of attention, and loving every minute of it. You're not still having doubts, are you, Josie?"

Josie laughed and shook her head, a huge feeling of relief washing over her. "Not a single one!" she said joyfully. "You know, I think Hope's last hope is going to be the best home she could possibly have!"

THE HORSESHOE TRILOGIES

Josie Grace grew up with Faith, Hope, and Charity, the horses at her family's riding school. Now that her family is forced to close the stables, she must find the horses new homes. If only she can find the perfect owners . . .

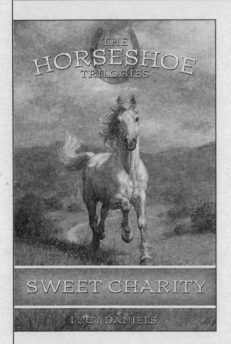

BOOK THREE:

SWEET CHARITY

Josie has loved Charity ever since the young horse was born at her family's riding stable. Charity is beautiful and spirited, and there is already a family interested in buying her—only Josie wishes she could keep Charity for herself. As the Graces prepare to move out of their house and away from the stables, Josie struggles to say good-bye to her favorite horse. But when Charity disappears from the stables one night, it is more than Josie can handle. Could Charity be gone forever?